D0986335

Mirror Mage

Dragon's Gift: The Huntress Book 2

Linsey Hall

Donated
to
Blue Ridge
Summit Library
In
Memory
Of
Marge Cox

Blue Ridge Summit Free Library
Box 34, 13676 Monterey Lane
Blue Ridge Summit, PA 17214

FRANKLIN COUNTY LIBRARY SYST
101 RAGGED EDGE ROAD SOUTH
CHAMBERSBURG, PA 17202

DEDICATION

For Judy and John Bowler, some of the most wonderful people I know who I love with all my heart.

SYST
ROAD SOUTH
SOS17 A9 .O   CHAMBER   101 RA

ACKNOWLEDGMENTS

The Dragon's Gift series is a product of my two lives: one as an archaeologist and one as a novelist. I'm fortunate to have friends from my other life who are experts on historical sites. I'd like to thank Dr. Ayse Devrim Atauz for her help with the ruins at Ephesus (the real life location of the final battle) and Julia, a Roman archaeologist for her help with the Roman brothel and prostitutes.

There was one aspect of combining my two lives that took a bit of work. I'd like to thank my friends, Wayne Lusardi, the State Maritime Archaeologist for Michigan, and Douglas Inglis and Veronica Morris, both archaeologists for Interactive Heritage, for their ideas about how to have a treasure hunter heroine that doesn't conflict too much with archaeology's ethics. The Author's Note contains a bit more about this if you are interested

Thank you, Ben, for everything you've done to support me in this career. Thank you to Carol Thomas for sharing your thoughts on the book and being amazing inspiration. My books are always better because of your help.

Thank you to Jena O'Connor and Lindsey Loucks for various forms of editing. The book is immensely better because of you!

GLOSSARY

Alpha Council - There are two governments that enforce law for supernaturals—the Alpha Council and the Order of the Magica. The Alpha Council governs all shifters. They work cooperatively with Alpha Council when necessary - for example, when capturing FireSouls.

ArchMage - The greatest mage of that particular skill. For example, the ArchMage of Fire Mages. There can also be an ArchWitch or ArchSorcerer.

Blood Sorceress - A type of Magica who can create magic using blood.

Conjurer - A Magica who uses magic to create something from nothing. They cannot create magic, but if there is magic around them, they can put that magic into their conjuration.

Dark Magic - The kind that is meant to harm. It's not necessarily bad, but it often is.

Deirfiúr - Sisters in Irish.

Demons - Often employed to do evil. They live in various hells but can be released upon the earth if you know how to get to them and then get them out. If they are killed on earth, they are sent back to their hell.

Dragon Sense - A FireSoul's ability to find treasure. It is an internal sense pulls them toward what they seek. It is easiest to find gold, but they can find anything or anyone that is valued by someone.

Elemental Mage – A rare type of mage who can manipulate all of the elements.

Enchanted Artifacts – Artifacts can be imbued with magic that lasts after the death of the person who put the magic into the artifact (unlike a spell that has not been put into an artifact—these spells disappear after the Magica's death). But magic is not stable. After a period of time—hundreds or thousands of years depending on the circumstance—the magic will degrade. Eventually, it can go bad and cause many problems.

Fire Mage – A mage who can control fire.

FireSoul - A very rare type of Magica who shares a piece of the dragon's soul. They can locate treasure and steal the gifts (powers) of other supernaturals. With practice, they can manipulate the gifts they steal, becoming the strongest of that gift. They are despised and feared. If they are caught, they are thrown in the Prison of Magical Deviants.

The Great Peace - The most powerful piece of magic ever created. It hides magic from the eyes of humans.

Half-blood - A supernatural who is half one species and half another. Example: shifter and Magica.

Heart of Glencarrough - The child who tends the Heartstone.

Hearth Witch – A Magica who is versed in magic relating to hearth and home. They are often good and potions and protective spells and are also very perceptive when on their own turf.

Heartstone - A charm that protects Glencarrough, the Alpha Council stronghold, from dark magic. It was created through the sacrifice of many shifters and must be tended by the Heart of Glencarrough, a child.

Magica - Any supernatural who has the power to create magic—witches, sorcerers, mages. All are governed by the Order of the Magica.

Mirror Mage - A Magica who can temporarily borrow the powers of other supernaturals. They can mimick the powers as long as the are near the other supernatural. Or they can hold onto the power, but once they are away from the other supernatural, they can only use it once.

The Origin - The descendent of the original alpha shifter. They are the most powerful shifter and can turn into any species.

Order of Holy Knowledge - A group of monks who collect and protect knowledge that live on an island in Ireland. They are supernaturals, but they do not use their powers.

Order of the Magica - There are two governments that enforce law for supernaturals—the Alpha Council and the Order of the Magica. The Order of the Magica govern all Magica. They work cooperatively with Alpha Council when necessary - for example, when capturing FireSouls.

Phantom - A type of supernatural that is similar to a ghost. They are incorporeal. They feed off the misery and pain of others, forcing them to relive their greatest nightmares and fears. They do not have a fully functioning mind like a human or supernatural. Rather, they are a shadow of their former selves. Half bloods are extraordinarily rare.

Scroll of Truths - A compendium of knowledge about the strongest supernaturals. It is a prophetic scroll that includes information about future powerful beings.

Seeker - A type of supernatural who can find things. FireSouls often pass off their dragon sense as being Seeker power.

Shifter - A supernatural who can turn into an animal. All are governed by the Alpha Council.

Transporter - A type of supernatural who can travel anywhere. Their power is limited and must regenerate after each use.

CHAPTER ONE

"Everyone knows you're not supposed to pick up the golden idol!" I shouted to Aidan as we sprinted down the dark corridor, deep within an ancient Mayan pyramid. The sound of jaguar paws thundered behind us.

Excuse me—*demon* jaguar paws. Far be it from me to forget exactly what chased me. Plain old jaguars wouldn't be guarding a treasure as valuable as the one I'd just stolen.

"Just because it almost bit Indiana Jones in the ass doesn't mean it'll bite us," Aidan said from beside me. "And you were the one who picked it up."

I grinned, loving that he'd caught my *Raiders of the Lost Ark* reference. My temporary tomb-raiding partner was more than qualified for the gig as my sidekick. I tightened my grip on the golden diadem I'd plucked off the pedestal in the treasure room we'd raided. I'd known it would set off a booby trap, but I'd done it anyway, of course.

To be clear, the jaguars were the booby trap—my own snarling, furry version of the giant boulder that had chased Indie through that temple in Peru.

"I think they're gaining on us," I panted as we sprinted toward the light at the end of the tunnel.

The exit was close enough that I could almost smell the humid jungle air. Only thirty more yards and those damn jaguars should go poof once they hit the sunlight. At least, that was how it normally worked with the enchantments guarding the tombs I raided.

The glowing exit beckoned.

A loud grinding noise filled the narrow corridor.

"Oh, hell," I muttered.

A massive stone door slowly lowered over the exit, cutting out the light.

I sucked a breath into my aching lungs and pushed myself faster, but it was a lost cause. The stone door was closing too quickly. It crashed to the ground.

Darkness. We were still ten yards away.

Damn. Stuck in a dead-end passage with six demon jaguars on our heels. I raised my hand, my lightstone ring flaring to life. A yellow glow poured over the gloomy tunnel.

"There!" Aidan pointed ahead.

My lightstone illuminated a narrow stone ledge over the blocked exit. We could fit on it. Barely. There was nowhere to go from there, but at least we'd have a sec to get our bearings and come up with a plan.

Assuming the jaguars couldn't jump that high.

I chanced a glance behind me. The jaguars were gaining, their emerald eyes glinting in the dim light. Short black horns poked out in front of their ears. These were not your average, oversized house cats.

"Yep!" I said. "Ledge looks good."

I'd jump onto pretty much anything to avoid those fangs.

"I'll toss you up," Aidan said as we neared it.

I eyed the ledge. If I took a running leap and used the side wall for leverage, I could probably make it. But it was damned tall. And the jaguars were *damned* fast. I had one chance, so why not use the services of the seriously built man at my side?

"All right," I said.

We skidded to a halt in front of the ledge. Aidan's big hands gripped my waist and he tossed me up. I grabbed the ledge and heaved myself onto the stone. Aidan pulled himself up behind me as the jaguars closed in. They leapt and snarled, their fangs gleaming in the light of my ring.

"Nice kitties," I cooed.

The biggest jaguar snarled and leapt so high his head was level with the stone ledge. I cringed, scrambling back.

"Yeah, that'll be the demon in them," I muttered. These were not normal jaguars.

"You're the one who thought this job would be a good opportunity to practice your magic, Cass," Aidan said, his deep voice making me shiver.

I glanced at him, struck anew at his dark good looks, then raised the diadem. "Yeah. This is worth a hell of a lot of money and the magic in it is almost decayed. A perfect find. Worth a little nip from one of these guys."

"A *little* nip?" He glanced down at the jaguars, his gray eyes skeptical.

"Fine, a big nip."

Aidan nodded. He was a big man, and all six feet-plus of him crowded me on the ledge. I tried to ignore the flicker of awareness. I'd only known him two weeks—since he'd hired me to find a dangerous scroll—and I'd developed a thing for him almost immediately. Like an addiction, but one I enjoyed even though I knew it was bad for me. Clearly I was crazy.

Just because we'd kissed once a week ago and I'd confirmed he was awesome at it didn't mean I had to get hot and bothered *all* the time. And this was clearly not the best moment.

"You haven't used your magic, you know." Censure colored his voice.

"Damn it." He was right. I was here to practice, not just find magic to stock my shop. As soon as I'd set off the jaguar booby trap by removing the diadem from its pedestal, I'd used my wits and speed rather than my magic.

"It's instinct not to use it," I said. "Keeping my power hidden is the only reason I've stayed alive all these years."

Normally I worked alone, but Aidan had come along because he was training me to use my magic, something I'd repressed all my life out of fear of being discovered as a FireSoul, the bogeyman of the supernatural world. I was hardly the bogeyman, but tell that to some scaredy-cat supernaturals and see how far it got you.

"I know. But something worse hunts you now." He nodded to the snarling jaguars. "Something that makes these guys look like kittens. The point of this job was so you could face a real threat with no witnesses."

"And stock my shop." But he was totally right. Practicing my magic was the priority. The Monster from my past hunted me. I didn't know his name, but I'd learned a week ago that he was still seeking me and my *deirfiúr*. My *deirfiúr*, Del and Nix, were my sisters by choice. If he caught me, I could kiss my life goodbye. And the lives of my *deirfiúr*. I needed to be strong enough to defeat him if—when—he found us.

The jaguars below continued to growl, their fangs flashing. Light shimmered around one, obscuring its form. When the glow faded, a tall demon stood in its place. The demon's skin was the same midnight shade as the jaguar's fur and his eyes an identical emerald green. White fangs peaked out from beneath his upper lip.

Excellent. The demon jaguars could shift. It made me feel less guilty about killing them. I didn't like killing animals, even ones out for my blood. But demons were fair game, and these jerks were just demons who could take the shape of a jaguar—all the better to catch and eat a tomb raider like myself.

"Come down from there, and we'll be nice and kill you quick." The demon's voice rumbled like the growl of a large cat.

"Yeah, I don't think so," I said.

"Use your Mirror Mage powers to shift," Aidan muttered. "I'll join you. We'll tear them apart."

My Mirror Mage powers allowed me to temporarily borrow the gifts of any supernatural around me. If I wanted, I could mimic the demon's ability to turn into a jaguar. Aidan, as the toughest Shifter of them all, could turn into a griffin. Together, we'd tear these guys apart.

Problem was, I was seriously out of practice with my magic, even after the five days I'd been training with Aidan. Shifting was one of the hardest things of all for me.

"I don't have a handle on shifting yet." Even so, I itched to try.

Below, a shimmer of light surrounded one of the other jaguars. A moment later, a tall demon stood in its place.

"Give me a boost," the demon said to the other as light began to glow around the remaining jaguars.

Damn it, they were all changing. They'd climb up here, and then it'd be hand-to-hand. I loved hand-to-hand—it was how I did most of my jobs—but this wasn't a normal job. This was magic practice.

And Aidan had insisted on taking my two trusty daggers so I'd be forced to practice my skills. I'd be demon chow without Lefty and Righty.

"Shift, Cass," Aidan demanded.

"No way. Too hard." I hadn't successfully completed the transition before, but Aidan was all about pushing my limits.

As an Elemental Mage in addition to being the most powerful Shifter in the known world, Aidan had elemental powers I could mirror, but I didn't want to start throwing stones around in a pyramid that could collapse on us. I could shoot fire from my fingers and turn them into demon barbecue, but that was too easy. I needed to challenge myself. That left one thing.

My FireSoul powers.

I thrust my hand toward the demons and envisioned lightning, bright and white. It flashed in my mind's eye, and the power crackled against my skin. The scent of ozone permeated the air.

The fizz and burn filled my chest, lighting me up like a livewire. It'd taken me all of the past week to master my new gift of lightning, but when I released the huge bolt, it cracked right into the middle of the demons. A direct hit. Adrenaline surged through me, joy on its heels.

It felt *good* to use my power.

Light flared and the ground quaked. *Damn.* I'd thrown too much power at them. The rock beneath their feet exploded, and shards of stone ricocheted toward us.

In a flash, Aidan curled his huge form around me, protecting me behind a wall of muscle. Normally, I'd be annoyed. I could protect myself, damn it. But I was so hopped up on the thrill of using my magic in a fight that I didn't care.

And this was the second time in two weeks that Aidan had thrown himself between me and a threat. I'd been peeved at him for coercing me into practicing my magic, but it was hard not to like a guy who put himself between you and danger.

Aidan jerked and grunted as flying stone hit him. Guilt chased away some of my power high. I hated hurting Aidan or causing damage to the pyramid. So far, I was 0 for 2.

"Sorry," I said. "Seems I still haven't got the lightning down either."

I really thought I'd mastered it. I'd practiced the new skill almost all week at Aidan's place, a remote estate in

Ireland where no one could see me or figure out what I was capable of.

"Still putting too much power into it," he muttered.

His breath was warm against my neck, the rumble of his voice a caress. I shivered. The power high and desire made my skin prickle with sensitivity. I ached to pull him toward me and confirm that he kissed as well as I remembered. The one we'd shared last week had been the best kiss I'd ever had with the hottest man I'd ever met.

Bad idea. I'd known him such a short time. And my life was too crazy right now for a relationship. There was a whole lot about Aidan I didn't know. He seemed too good to be true, and in my life, that'd always been a red flag.

"I think we're good," I said, pushing at his hard chest. "Rubble's not flying anymore."

"I kind of like this position," Aidan said.

Desire tugged at me. I liked it too. This was the first time since our kiss that he'd been so close to me.

Really bad idea.

I shoved him and he moved. "Yeah, well, if I haven't zapped those demons, you're not going to like it for long."

I peered over the ledge. My lightning had gouged away part of the stone floor and wall. Guilt pierced me. This place was old as hell, and I'd screwed it up. It'd been fine for a thousand years, and then I came along and *bam!* There's a giant hole in the entrance. There was a customer waiting on this diadem and we needed the fee pronto, but I'd have to come back and fix this when I returned the diadem.

The demons—all of them in their demon forms—lay scattered like fallen bowling pins below. A satisfied grin stretched across my face, nudging out some of the guilt.

Dead.

Sort of. You couldn't really kill demons. After death on earth, they regenerated in their hell. But they wouldn't be giving us trouble anytime soon. Lightning was a hell of a gift to have.

It was the only gift I'd ever used my FireSoul powers to steal, though I didn't technically steal it. I've always owned up to being a Mirror Mage. That was acceptable in the world of magic because I only borrowed the gifts. But if the Order of the Magica or the Alpha Council found out I was also a FireSoul, they'd toss me in the Prison for Magical Miscreants to rot to death. Their fear was understandable. A FireSoul had to kill to steal magical gifts. We were the only species who could do so. One power-hungry FireSoul could cause a hell of a lot of damage.

"Looks like you got them," Aidan said.

"Yeah. Let's get out of here." I cradled the delicate diadem to my chest and jumped down from the ledge, avoiding the crispy demons at my feet. Their bodies would disappear soon, returning to their hells. Thank magic, because I really didn't want to clean them up. Their scent gagged me. "They stink, and this thing needs to get back to my shop."

Aidan's big form thudded to the ground next to me. "Agreed. How about you get us out of here."

I turned to the rock slab that acted as a door. He could move it in the blink of an eye, but that wasn't the point of this exercise. I had to do it.

"No problem." I reached out for Aidan's Elemental Mage abilities. His power seethed against mine, immensely strong and vibrant. He was one of the most powerful Magica in the world, not to mention the Origin, a descendent of the original Shifter Alpha. A scary bastard, when you got down to it.

When I was near him, I could borrow whatever power I wanted. That made me a scary bastard too. Though I liked to think of myself as one anyway.

When I consciously reached out for Aidan's magic, it lit up my senses. The smell of evergreen, the sound of roaring waves, and the taste of dark chocolate hit me. It was a warm caress against my skin, like a massage or a bubble bath. Supernaturals could feel the magic in others, but only strong supernaturals like Aidan gave off signatures for all five senses. Normally, he controlled and hid his signature, but when I accessed his magic, I could sense it.

Mentally, I shifted through his magic. I had to ignore what his power made me feel and sort through the various Magica gifts he possessed. His ability over water felt like raindrops against my skin. I bypassed it. I also bypassed the heat of flame and the gust of air. When I touched upon his gift of power over stone, it felt like rough dry rocks under my fingertips. I grasped hold of it. Power zinged down to my fingertips, and I raised my hands and directed my fingers at the stone. Magic flowed from them.

The sound of thousands of pounds of stone grinding against stone filled the dim corridor as the rock slab rose slowly. The strip of bright sunlight at the bottom widened. I squinted against the blazing light as the Mexican jungle came into view.

"Not bad," Aidan said. "You're control is getting better."

"Thanks." I couldn't help the grin that stretched over my face. Every other time I'd borrowed other people's powers, I'd been in an adrenaline-fueled panic to save my life or someone else's. I usually got the job done, but my control was limited. See Exhibit A: Exploding Stone Floor from five minutes ago.

My smile faded at the reminder of my lightning power and what it'd taken for me to get it. Aaron, a FireSoul like me, had been a slave to the Monster from my past. I'd met him a week ago, while we'd been fighting over the scroll that Aidan had hired me to find. Aaron had given me his gift of lightning right before he'd died—willingly, he'd said—though I still felt guilty.

"I still don't get why you're helping me," I said. I was such a risk.

We walked out into the jungle. The mid-afternoon sun pounded down, the heat soaking into my skin as the humid air filled my lungs. "It's a big risk for you. If the Order of the Magica or the Alpha Council find out you're harboring a FireSoul, you could get tossed in prison as well."

"Because I like you, Cass. A lot. I'm not afraid of the Order of the Magica or the Alpha Council. They're not going to stop me from trying to help you. You need your power if you're going to defeat the Monster who hunts you. I saw how dangerous he can be. I know you've hidden your gifts because you're afraid of being thrown in the Prison for Magical Miscreants, but the man who hunts you is a bigger threat."

The thud and rumble of the plane's wheels hitting the runway jerked me out of sleep. I lurched upright in the plush seat and dragged my hand over my mouth.

Oh, crap. Had I been drooling?

Maybe, but at least Aidan had his head buried in a book in the seat across the aisle. His private plane was otherwise empty, as usual. We'd hiked out of the jungle, driven to the nearest airstrip, jumped onboard this swanky tin can, and about eight hours later were landing in my home of Magic's Bend, Oregon.

It was one of the few concealed, all-magic cities in the world, hidden by an enormous spell called the Great Peace. Humans who approached would veer away. The spell also kept humans from seeing our magic, though they could see us if we were in their spaces.

Which I often was while traveling to and from my job as a magic hunter for the shop I owned with my *deirfiúr*. It was still surreal to be traveling to and from jobs in a private plane. We could fly to the closest airstrip near the temple or tomb I was supposed to raid and be in and out in a day. Way different than my usual method of flying coach and taking public transport through some seriously remote places.

Traveling with Aidan Merrick, the Origin and founder of Origin Enterprises, was way better than being crammed into a bus between a lady with a chicken and someone's pig. Apparently owning a security company was lucrative.

"What time is it?" I asked.

"About 7:00 p.m. You passed out as soon as we took off."

No surprise. Using my magic still made me tired. The more practiced I became, the less exhausted I would be. Unfortunately, I wasn't very practiced yet.

It didn't take us long to get off the plane—another perk of flying private—and the cool breeze cleared the sleep from my head. I'd lived in the all-magical city with my *deirfiúr* for the last five years. Though I'd been staying in a guest room at Aidan's estate in Ireland for the last five days to practice my magic, we'd had to come to Oregon to deliver the diadem to Ancient Magic, my shop.

There was only one car on the tarmac, the same large black SUV Aidan drove when he was in Magic's Bend. An assistant, a tall guy with dark hair, stood next to it.

"I can catch a cab to my place if you just want to head home," I said.

Aidan had a few houses I knew of, though I'd only ever been to the one in Ireland. He also had a place in Magic's Bend. On the wealthy side of town, of course. Far from my own side.

"I'll take you home," Aidan said. "I don't like the idea of you being on your own."

"I'm not on my own. I've got Lefty and Righty." I patted the thigh holsters holding my obsidian knives. I'd insisted he return them as soon as we got back on the plane. "And I'll be with my *deirfiúr* as soon as I get back to Factory Row."

"You need to stop leaning on your fighting skills and practice your magic," Aidan said as we made our way across the tarmac to his car.

"I hear you, but there's no way in hell I'm practicing in a city full of supernaturals." It was one thing to use my magic in an abandoned pyramid that only held demons. But in a city? "If one person gets a whiff of what I am, they'd be scared shitless. They could turn me over to the Alpha Council or the Order of the Magica and probably get themselves a nice bounty."

Working hard to access your magic was a lot like sweating. You gave off more of your magical signature for other supernaturals to sense. Until I was well practiced, I needed to try not to access my power around others.

"You'll become better," Aidan said as we climbed into his car. "With more practice, you'll be able to keep others from sensing what you are. You can pass your gifts off as Mirror Mage powers."

"Yeah, as long as they don't catch me before I'm good enough to hide the truth." That'd take time. I'd used so much magic over these last two weeks that I was completely on edge. It was super unlikely anyone had seen me—I'd stuck to Aidan's private property and other remote areas—but it was hard to shake the paranoia and fear that had followed me for ten years.

"You'll get good enough."

The faith in his voice hit me hard. I shouldn't care what he thought of me. He was just a guy, after all. I didn't have space in my life for guys. Especially not handsome, powerful, kind ones who seemed to be nothing but good. Contrary to what it sounded like, those kinds of guys were *actually* nothing but trouble. You could fall for one of those guys.

For a girl who could trust no one but her *deirfiúr*, that was dangerous. Neither my *deirfiúr* nor I remembered the first fifteen years of our life. We'd woken in a field at fifteen with a single memory each: that we were FireSouls, we were running from someone, and that person wanted to hurt us. That person *had* been hurting us, because we were FireSouls.

As a result, Nix, Del, and I had moved around so much prior to settling in Magic's Bend five years ago that I'd learned not to grow attached to anyone else. You would eventually have to leave them behind. If the Monster caught up to us, we'd have to run again.

But I was an adult now. If I wanted to make this work, I might be able to. Though I'd be lying if I said the idea didn't scare the crap out of me. What if Aidan actually was as great as he seemed? That'd sure as hell be hard to ignore.

"Here we are."

Aidan's deep voice startled me out of my thoughts. The tall brick faces of the buildings on Factory Row loomed outside the car, their large windows like great black eyes in the night. Apparently I'd zoned out hard during the drive.

I grabbed the small box containing the diadem and climbed out of the car. I pulled my small bag off the floor and said, "Thanks for the ride. I'll see you tomorrow. Eight, right?"

We were planning to head back to Ireland to practice my magic. As much as I told myself I didn't want to go, I was lying. Not only was he right that I needed the practice, but I wanted to be around him. No matter how dumb it was.

"I'll walk you in." He climbed out of the car.

"You don't have to."

"Call me cautious. Last time we were here, the shop was in the middle of a break-in."

The thief—Aaron, the FireSoul who'd eventually given me his power—had still been inside. Only that time, he'd been working on behalf of the Monster. He'd caused a hell of a lot of damage.

"Thanks." I turned to face my building.

The windows of Ancient Magic were dark. It was long past closing time. While I was out hunting artifacts, my sister Nix ran the shop. She was the Protector. When Del, my other sister, wasn't off hunting demons for bounty, she used archives to identify the magic we wanted to sell that was stored in artifacts. Del was the Seeker. I then hunted the magic artifacts, which made me the Huntress. We made a good team.

We crossed the street to Ancient Magic. The night was quiet save for the chirp of crickets in the park across from the converted factories. Factory Row was the recently gentrified part of Magic's Bend and was the perfect location for our shop and the apartments we occupied above because it was both spacious and cheap.

I reached the glass door and ran my hands over the exterior edges. The fizz of magic tingled on my palms as the enchantment faded. Only my *deirfiúr* or myself could disarm it. Though the door looked like nothing more than glass, if you weren't one of us, there was no way to get through. During opening hours, that wasn't the case. Anyone could walk in. It'd be a pretty crap shop if customers couldn't enter.

I stepped through the door and flicked on the light. The sight of the half-empty shelves dragged at my heart.

"Place looks better," Aidan said.

"I guess. A lot less broken glass, at least. But inventory is down by more than half." I walked to the front counter and put the artifact on the processing shelf behind it. We'd have trouble with rent because of the diminished inventory.

We didn't actually sell the artifacts I found. That was illegal. What we sold was the magic the enchanted artifacts contained. We removed it from the artifact, put it into a replica, and returned the original to the site where I'd found it. Without magic to sell...

Well, we needed money to make rent. And fast. This might be the cheap part of town, but we'd rented out the whole building, most of it for our personal, dragon-inspired troves of treasure that we kept secret. FireSouls were said to share part of a dragon's soul, though no one had seen a dragon in millennia. I possessed the dragon's covetousness and was compelled to keep a trove of my own treasure. For me, it was leather jackets, weapons, and boots. Weird, yeah, but I couldn't help myself.

"You hungry?" Aidan asked.

My stomach growled in response, as if it knew English too.

"I'll take that as a yes. Let's head to Potions & Pastilles. I'll get you a pasty."

"I'd think you'd be sick of me by now."

"It'll be a long while before I'm sick of you." His dark gray gaze met mine. The heat in it made me shiver and wonder when he'd get sick of waiting for me.

The dumb part of me hoped he'd snap and drag me into his arms and kiss me. I shoved that part down deep and said, "Sure. I agreed to meet Nix and Del there anyway."

"Good." He grinned.

Damn it, why did he have to be so handsome? And smart and kind?

We headed out, and Aidan waited while I reengaged the enchantments by running my hands around the edges of the door. Light rain began to fall as we walked down the street to the coffee shop run by two of my friends, Claire and Connor.

Fortunately, it was only twenty yards down the way, and we weren't too wet by the time we arrived. Yellow light gleamed from the windows as we approached, the sight filling me with warmth. This place was probably more my home than my own apartment, which I used just for sleeping and hiding my trove.

Aidan pushed open the door, and I couldn't help the sigh that escaped me when the scent of Cornish Pasties enveloped me. The kitchen was small at P & P's, but Connor made a mean Cornish Pasty in the small space. They'd moved here from Cornwall a year before we'd arrived and hadn't been able to leave that part of their home behind.

And I was grateful. Without them, I wouldn't be able to continue my half-decade-long love affair with the savory treat. It was the most exciting action I'd gotten in a while, actually, besides Aidan's kiss.

"Hey! Took you long enough." Del waved from her comfy leather seat in the corner. Her black hair was pulled back, and her blue eyes gleamed with welcome. Nix smiled at me, then jerked her head toward Aidan and made a face that said, "How's it going with your guy?"

I glowered.

They sat in our usual spot. P & P was a coffee shop/whiskey bar, depending on the hour of the day. There were about half a dozen small wooden tables in the middle and comfy chairs scattered around the perimeter.

"Yeah, yeah," I said to Del. "Let me order, and I'll be right over."

I followed Aidan to the small counter bar at the back. My friend Connor stood behind it, dressed in his usual band t-shirt and jeans with his dark hair flopped over his brow. He was busy putting the finishing touches on a whiskey cocktail. Besides enchanted coffees, P & P's sold a variety of whiskeys at night. Connor's idea, but it'd been a good one, as it drew in a whole different crowd in the evenings. There were at least half a dozen couples or small groups in the space.

"Hey, guys." Connor grinned as he glanced up. "Be right with you."

He handed off the cocktail to the pretty Shifter who stood at the far end of the bar, then turned to us.

"Long time no see," Connor said. "Where you been hiding?"

"Just working on a tricky job," I said.

Even though he and Claire were my closest friends besides my *deirfiúr*, they didn't know I was a FireSoul. There was no point telling Connor I'd been at Aidan's, practicing my magic. I should feel guilty about the secrets, but I honestly couldn't feel too bad about it. It might make me a bad person, but keeping my *deirfiúr* and myself safe always came first. And the secret actually protected Connor. This way, he wasn't knowingly harboring a FireSoul.

"What'll it be, then?" Connor asked. "Whiskey for you, Aidan? I've got a new one in from Oban."

"Perfect." Aidan grinned. "And the pasty of the day."

"PBR for me," I said. "And two pasties."

Connor scrunched his brow. "You still drink that stuff?"

"Oh, come on. You know I do. I'm not betraying my one true beer love for any of that fancy craft stuff."

He laughed. "All right, all right. Hang on."

He poured Aidan's whiskey, pulled a can of PBR out of the little fridge, then handed them over. "Your hipster beer, madam. I'll bring the pasties out after I've warmed them up."

"Hillbilly beer," I corrected as I pulled a few crumpled bills out of my pocket.

Aidan beat me to it, handing over a crisp fifty. "I've got it."

I frowned at him, then remembered the catastrophe at Ancient Magic. Del, Nix, and I were going to have a hard time paying the bills until we found enough magic in enchanted artifacts to refill our stock. Even Del had started hunting artifacts when she didn't have a demon to track down. We could sell off the treasures in our respective troves, but parting with any of our preciouses would be damned hard.

So, I said, "Thanks. I'll get you next time."

"Hardly necessary."

"Just because you're loaded doesn't mean I'm going to let you pay the bills. This isn't a date."

"But it could be, if you agreed to one."

I shivered. Dates usually involved kissing. At least at the end. His dark eyes promised at least kissing. As much as I wanted to sign up for that…

"Bad idea," I said as I turned and walked toward my *deirfiúr*.

Though Aidan always walked on silent feet, I could feel him behind me. His gaze heated my back. I took a seat in front of my *deirfiúr*.

Nix's green gaze met mine. Today, she wore the usual ripped jeans and motorcycle boots, but her T-shirt of the day proclaimed her a ball-collecting feminist. I grinned.

"How'd it go?" she asked.

"Got the diadem," I said. "I put it behind the counter. It's ready for you whenever."

"I'll do it as soon as I leave here. The buyer wants it pronto. She needs to be beautiful for some TV thing. You can take the original back to the pyramid any time after that."

In addition to protecting the shop, Nix was in charge of transferring the magic in each artifact. She used her skills as a Conjurer to create the replicas of the artifacts, then transferred the original artifact's magic to the replica, which we sold.

"Great." I glanced at Del. "You get the sword?"

She nodded. "The magic in it was almost decayed, but Nix managed to stabilize it when she transferred it to the replica."

With time, magic decayed and destabilized. By taking the magic out of the old artifacts, we were saving the artifacts from destruction.

"It'll make some wimp a great fighter when he wields it," Nix said.

"Perfect."

Each artifact housed a different type of spell. Ones that improved fighting skills were often hot items. We'd sell it for a pretty penny soon.

"But I've got a lead on a demon who has a big bounty on his head," Del said. "I'm going after him later. Shouldn't take long to bag him. I've got a contact who says he knows where the demon hunts at dawn."

"What kind of demon?" Aidan asked.

"Rylon. A baby eater." Del's face twisted with menace.

My stomach pitched. There were all kinds of demons from all kinds of hells. They shouldn't be roaming the earth because they weren't good at keeping a low profile around humans, but they were often in places they shouldn't be. The Order of the Magica offered a bounty to those who caught them. Fortunately, Del was good at catching them.

"Good luck," I said.

"Best pasties you'll ever taste!"

My friend Claire's cheerful voice sounded from behind me. I turned. Claire approached with a tray of pasties. She was wearing her fighting leathers, which meant she'd just come from one of her mercenary jobs, but she wasn't covered in blood, so her brother had clearly roped her into helping with P & P.

"Thanks." I almost moaned at the delicious smell wafting from the pasties—savory beef and potatoes wrapped in buttery pastry. I bit into one, not caring that it was too hot, and glanced up at Claire. "You kill whatever you were after?"

"You know it. A rogue Shifter who was going after Magica in his wolf form."

"Weird."

Though they don't really trust each other, Shifters and Magica got along all right. Despite our different magical skill sets—Magica *did* magic, whereas Shifters *were* magic—we were about equal in a fight because Shifters were partially immune to magic when in their animal form. It would take a hell of a lot of my lightning to bring down a Shifter, and in the meantime, they could get to me and chew my head right off. But the lightning would still hurt like hell, and I might get off enough bolts to kill a Shifter before they got to me, so Shifters usually didn't want to fight us any more than we wanted to fight them.

"At least you got him," Del said.

"Yep. And now all I want to do is shower, but little brother is a slave driver." She scowled back toward the kitchen.

I laughed and damn, it felt good. It might have been the first time I'd laughed since I'd realized the man from my nightmares—the Monster—was coming for us. It reminded me that life was good. No matter what our current problems, we could get back on track. Whatever hunted us, we'd face it.

The door opened behind me, and a gust of cool wind blew into the shop. The smell of rain followed it. I turned to see if it was still coming down, but a big man loomed in the doorway. I stiffened.

Mathias. His wild golden hair and hulking size betrayed his Shifter species—lion. I'd met him a week ago when I'd needed help finding the Scroll of Truths. He'd been the lover of the woman I'd gone to for help, a blood sorceress named Mordaca.

His yellow gaze landed on me, and recognition flared in his eyes. He strode toward our group, bringing with him the scent of his magic. Dry, like the desert or the planes of Africa.

He stopped in front of our cluster of chairs and turned to Aidan. He bowed low, a gesture of respect to the strongest of all Shifters. "Origin."

The deep regard in his voice hit me. I'd forgotten how the Shifters felt about the Origin. He was almost a god to them.

Aidan nodded. "Mathias."

Mathias rose and turned to me. "Cassiopeia Clereaux. The Alpha Council is looking for you."

My stomach felt like it had dropped right out of my body and all the breath left my lungs. The Alpha Council was looking for me? That made no sense, unless they knew what I was.

I tried to keep my face impassive as my mind raced. Had Mathias figured out what I was when I'd gone to Mordaca for help? Had he told his government I was a FireSoul? They didn't govern Magica—my kind—but they hunted FireSouls, just like the Order of the Magica, because we could steal their shifting ability if we killed them. We were a danger to everyone, Shifter, Magica, or any supernatural in between.

Sharp metal bit into my fingers. I glanced down. My hand was fisted around my now dented beer can, and a ridge of metal cut into my finger. Slowly, I drew in a breath and lowered the can to my side so no one could see it.

"Yeah?" I asked, trying to appear calm.

A glance at my *deirfiúr* showed that Nix was white as snow, her brown hair standing out starkly against her skin, and Del was turning the faintest shade of blue. She was so freaked out she was starting to turn into her phantom form.

Not good.

When I'd started practicing my magic, this was what I'd been afraid of. One of the two governing bodies catching wind of what I was and coming after me.

"Why is the Alpha Council looking for me?"

Mathias glanced at Aidan. "Aidan told us about your skills."

Fear and rage clashed within me as my gaze jerked to Aidan. *He'd told them what I was?*

CHAPTER TWO

"We need your help," Mathias continued.

Confused, I dragged my gaze back to him. "My help?"

If they knew I was a FireSoul, wouldn't they just arrest me?

"Yes. When we came to him with our problem, Aidan said that you're the best Seeker in Magic's Bend and that you could help us. The Alpha Council has lost something of great value. Mordaca attempted to help find it, but she failed. We hope that you will try."

I swallowed hard. So they didn't know I was a FireSoul? My ability to find anything of value was due to my dragon sense, but I passed myself off in public as being part Seeker, a type of Magica that was also good at finding things.

Or was this a trick?

"What are you looking for?" I asked.

"I am not authorized to share that information with you. You must come to Glencarrough, our stronghold, and speak directly with the Alpha Council."

"I'm sorry, I don't begin jobs without knowing what I'm looking for."

And no way was I going into the Shifter stronghold. The protections on that place were legendary. Both the Alpha Council and the Order of the Magica lived in strongholds that made Fort Knox look like it was constructed of Legos and had security provided by a crack team of kittens. There was *no* way to get in without permission. And once you were in, there was no way to get out.

No way in frozen hell was I going in there. I glanced at my *deirfiúr*. Their faces pretty much said the same.

A frown creased Mathias's brow. He was handsome in a hulking, leonine way. Nothing like Aidan, who looked like a male model who sold rugged things like hiking equipment, but handsome all the same.

"We've heard what happened to your shop, Ancient Magic," Mathias said. "We understand that much of you inventory was destroyed. We'll pay you a million dollars to come have a meeting with the Alpha Council. To hear them out. If you take the job, we will pay you a million more."

The breath almost whooshed out of my lungs. That was a *lot* of money. I glanced at my *deirfiúr*. Their eyes were wide as well.

We needed that money. Not just to pay our bills, but to continue feeding our troves. Two million dollars would go a long way toward padding my collection. Would I put myself in danger for that?

Even though the rational part of myself wanted to say *of course not*, the reality was that my trove was more of an addiction than a pleasure. The idea that I would risk my life for a collection of leather jackets and knives was embarrassing, but it was true. The covetousness in Del and Nix's eyes confirmed the same about them.

But it wasn't just a dangerous job. If they knew what I was...

Fear shocked some sense into me. "I'm sorry. I can't take the job."

Mathias's blond brows rose. "Really? It's a million dollars just for a meeting, and you won't go?"

When he put it like that, it did sound suspicious. If I weren't hiding something, I'd have no problem meeting with the Alpha Council.

"My job is lucrative. I no longer make decisions based on the fee." Now *that* was a big fat lie, but I had to get out of this. It wasn't worth the risk.

"There are lives at stake." Mathias's voice was low, almost anguished. But it was his gaze that got me. Haunted. Afraid.

"Lives?" I frowned.

"Yeah. I need you to take this meeting. Hear us out."

Oh, hell. "Can you give us a minute?"

He nodded and walked to the counter. Once he began speaking to Connor, I turned to Aidan and my *deirfiúr*.

"Why the did you tell them about me?" I hissed at Aidan.

"I didn't tell them your secret. But they do need help. Badly. Like he said, lives are at risk. And if you do this job, you'll be on their good side. That could come in very handy if you're ever discovered."

Damn it, he was right. I wanted to be pissed at him—and I was—but he had a point.

I glanced at Nix and Del. "It's risky, but proving myself as honorable and helpful to the Alpha Council will give us a strong ally in the event shit ever hits the fan."

Nix nodded. "This is so risky. But that's worth more than the money."

"Which is worth a hell of a lot," Del said.

I leaned toward Aidan, bouncing my leg in fear and anticipation. "Lives really are at risk?"

"Yes." His gaze was serious.

"And you swear they don't know what I am?" I whispered.

"It's highly unlikely. I didn't tell them, so they'd have to guess."

"You guessed," I said.

"I spent a week with you under extraordinary circumstances." He flicked imaginary lint off his sleeve. "And I'm a genius."

I scowled. I didn't know about the genius part, but he was right. The trials we'd gone through to get to the scroll had forced me to reveal my powers. I'd agreed to help him find the scroll because it contained the names of the most powerful supernaturals, myself included. It would have blown my secret if he or anyone else had read it. Instead, I'd blown my own secret by using my magic around him.

But he hadn't figured out that my *deirfiúr* were FireSouls as well, because I'd told him the scroll had been destroyed. It was actually locked away in my trove. I should have felt guilty about hiding it from Aidan, but I didn't. Protecting my *deirfiúr* and myself always came first. It was why I'd told him almost nothing about my past.

"Fine. I'll meet with the Alpha Council. But since I can't be guaranteed they don't know what I am"—I couldn't repress the shiver of fear—"you have to go with me and provide backup. They respect you, right? They'd do what you say?"

He nodded sharply. "Yes."

"What if one of them senses the strength of my magic?"

"They shouldn't. Your magic is better hidden than you think. Even I couldn't sense it when I met you," he said.

"But I've been using it so much lately. It's no longer dormant within me."

"True. But I only sense it when you use it. As long as you don't use it there, they shouldn't be able to sense it. Just stay close to me. We'll pass it off as my magic if necessary. They won't question me."

I let out a shuddery breath. It wasn't a guarantee of safety, but it wasn't bad either.

I looked at Del and Nix. Like all things, we were in this together. "You're cool with this?"

"It's risky," Nix said. She'd always been the cautious one. "But if people are depending on you… That's hard to ignore."

"I think you should do it," Del said. "If you can get the Alpha Council to owe us one, that can only be a good thing. And two million bucks... Not that we should risk our lives for that, but..."

"Hard to resist." I thought of all the things I could put in my trove with that kind of money. It was a dumb thought, but if the shoe fits...

I looked at Aidan. "Can you give us a moment?"

His gray gaze searched mine, but eventually he nodded and got up. Once he'd reached the bar and begun to talk to Mathias, I turned back to my *deirfiúr*.

"You guys really trust Aidan? I thought you were wary of him after the battle with Aaron."

"Yeah, and I'm still kinda iffy. But don't you trust him?" Nix asked. "You just spent a week at his place."

"Only because he threatened to reveal what I am if I didn't practice my magic. And his place is the safest place to practice."

"Because he cares about you," Del said. "I've only known the guy a couple weeks, and even I can see that. He knows what hunts us and he's right—having control of your magic is the only way to defeat the Monster. I know you're wary of yours because it was so powerful and out of control for so long, but we need all of us operating at full strength."

I sighed. They were right. Both Del and Nix had a pretty good handle on their magic—they always had. Nix was a Conjurer, and Del was a Traveler/Phantom Hybrid. They both had more to learn, but at least they didn't blow things up when they used their gifts. It'd allowed them to practice all these years while I'd been hiding.

Ever since I'd woken with no memories at fifteen, my own magic had been uncontrollable. I hadn't been able to practice it out of fear that other supernaturals would notice how strong I was. And because I frequently blew things up when I tried to use my magic.

"Fine. I'll do the job."

They both nodded, satisfied.

I got up and went to the bar.

Aidan and Mathias leaned against it, chatting about baseball of all things. Though Mathias was a big guy who radiated danger like any lion Shifter would, he paled in comparison to Aidan. Not only was Aidan taller, but the feeling of danger that rolled off him was hard to ignore.

So was the strength of his magic. Though I was trying to learn to contain my signature, Aidan wasn't as worried about people knowing his strength. He was already famous as the Origin, the descendent of the original shifter. People might as well know he could also kick their ass with his Elemental Mage abilities. Or tear their heads off as a griffin.

Thank magic the guy was on my side.

The two men turned to face me, one golden and one dark. Worry creased Mathias's brow. Whatever was plaguing the Shifters, he really wanted my help with it.

"I'll take the meeting," I said. "Depending on the job, I may take that as well."

Some of the grimness faded from his eyes. "Thank you. We have a plane waiting at Fairfield Airport."

I stiffened. I didn't like the idea of being trapped on their plane. It was silly because I'd be walking straight into their stronghold soon, but I couldn't help it.

33

"We'll take mine," Aidan said. "And we'll meet you there tomorrow afternoon."

I relaxed a little. Fates, I was a lucky girl. Not only had Aidan agreed to watch my back when we went to Glencarrough, he sensed when I was nervous and offered his plane. His freaking plane. How was this my life?

"Thank you," Mathias said. "Until then."

I nodded and watched him leave, then turned back to Aidan. Connor had gone into the kitchen and the back of the coffee shop had cleared out, so we were alone.

"You look bothered," Aidan said.

I looked up to meet his gaze, hating that he was so much taller and stronger than me. It was sexy, yeah, but I was so off balance around him. All my life, my *deirfiúr* and I had kept our distance from anyone more powerful than us, hoping that it would help keep us safe. It had worked. Except for the fact that I was now woefully underprepared for dealing with someone like Aidan.

"I don't get you," I said. "You show up in my life, learn what I am, and instead of turning me in, you help me. Even your freaking heavy-handedness in making me practice my magic seems to be for my own safety. You're too good to be true."

Shadows fell over his face. "I wish that were the case, but you don't know enough about me to say that."

He was right. I didn't. I knew that he'd built his company and his fortune himself, that he was the descendent of the original Shifter, that he was the strongest supernatural I'd ever met, and that he appeared to be a decent guy, but I'd only known him two weeks.

I'd barely asked anything about him during that time. And people didn't come out and say all their bad shit to you right off the bat.

"So there is some bad stuff?" I asked.

"There's bad stuff about everyone, Cass." Aidan's voice was weary. "But I don't let it define me."

"What's your bad stuff?" I couldn't begin to guess, but someone as wealthy and powerful as he was would've had plenty of opportunities to screw up. I didn't know if it made me feel better or worse. From his dark expression, I should probably feel worse.

The wooden door to the kitchen swung open, and Connor bustled out, two plates of pasties in his hands. He grinned when he saw us. "Be right with you guys."

The moment was broken. Aidan's face had returned to its normal, impassive state and he said, "We'll need to leave for Scotland tonight if we're going to reach Glencarrough by tomorrow afternoon."

"Scotland?" The location of the Alpha Council stronghold was a secret, but given the name Glencarrough, it made sense.

"Yes. The jet should be refueled soon. If you want to pack a fresh bag, I can pick you up in an hour. I need to swing by my place for a change of clothes."

"All right."

I watched him walk out of the coffee shop, his stride that of a man confident in his place at the top of the mountain. I wasn't used to relationships. Growing close to anyone besides my *deirfiúr* while I harbored such a dangerous secret was a terrible idea. I certainly didn't have experience with guys like Aidan.

And I didn't know how to deal with someone besides my *deirfiúr* knowing what I was. I'd wanted to trust someone else with the truth, to not always hide behind my lies, but now that I had that opportunity, it made me uncomfortable as hell.

A week ago, I thought I was just mad at him for forcing me to confront my powers. Now, I realized I was probably more afraid than mad. And I hated being afraid.

CHAPTER THREE

"That's where the Alpha Council lives?" I asked as our Range Rover descended into the valley.

Mountains rose up on either side, surrounding the enormous stone structure crouched in between them. It was a monstrosity of towers and walls that spread across the valley in central Scotland.

"Appropriate, don't you think?" Aidan asked as he drove us down the narrow road. Sheep scurried out of the way, their little white legs kicking up as they bounded away.

"Sure, for a horror movie about a haunted castle and its not-so-friendly ghost." I surveyed the gray stone and the fantastical architecture. The size and complexity was mind-boggling. Once inside, you were only getting out if they let you. I rubbed my sweaty palms against my jeans.

"It's kept them safe for hundreds of years. No reason to leave."

I could think of a few. It looked so lonely and creepy. The desolate beauty of the Highlands didn't help. Despite the late afternoon sun, the place looked like something out of a fairytale. But it was the villain's castle.

We'd been driving for two hours now, ever since landing at the nearest airstrip in a small village. I'd slept almost the entire flight, still exhausted from using my magic, but I'd been wound tight since we'd gotten into the car.

I'd never willingly gone into a place full of government officials—either Order of the Magica or Alpha Council—and though I knew I'd had a good reason for coming here, I was having a hard time remembering it.

"It'll be all right," Aidan said.

Damn. He'd noticed I was freaked out. "Yeah, it'll be fine."

I tried to play it cool as he slowed the car to a halt in front of a soaring wooden gate. I leaned over and looked up, craning my neck to see the tops of the walls. At least a dozen faces peered down at me, all scowling.

"That's a lot of guards," I said.

"There's more on my side."

"Weird. You'd think they'd use magic instead of manpower to guard the gates. This is so…so human."

"Yeah, it's off all right."

A familiar face appeared at the top of the wall. Wild golden hair blew in the summer wind and yellow eyes met mine through the glass. Mathias. He turned and waved a hand, presumably to someone in charge of the gate.

With a groaning noise, the heavy wooden door lifted. My stomach sank with every inch it rose. We were driving straight into the lion's den, bad pun intended. There would be dozens, maybe even hundreds, of

Shifters here. Shifters who were largely immune to my magic. Outnumbered didn't begin to describe my situation.

Aidan directed the Range Rover into an enormous courtyard, and I tried to still my bouncing leg.

Though the exterior had suggested a medieval courtyard full of dirty villagers and ponies wandering on packed dirt, I didn't see that. Instead, everything looked modern. Cars were parked neatly in a cobblestone courtyard, and large stone buildings loomed at the edges, their glass windows winking in the sun.

Mathias descended the stone steps. He wore jeans and a dark sweater. Though he should look civilized, the wild hair and golden eyes gave him a hint of animal. He pointed one big hand toward the largest building at the back.

Unable to help myself, I ran my hand over the dagger strapped to my right thigh as Aidan pulled into a parking space in front of the building Mathias had indicated. When he killed the engine, silence loomed. My heartbeat pounded in my ears.

"No need for that." Aidan eyed my hand near my knife.

I clenched my fist. "Habit."

"You need to learn to reach for your magic when you're nervous."

"Yeah, yeah." But he was right.

I sucked in a deep breath and climbed out of the car, trying to keep the tension from showing on my face. I just had to play it cool, that was all. Easy peasy.

Right.

I could feel the magic in the air here. Taste it and smell it. No one here was as powerful as Aidan, but so many Shifters in one area gave the place a buzzing feeling. The scents of animals, some good and some bad, hit me, even though I saw none in their shifted form.

Mathias approached and bowed low to Aidan. When he straightened, he looked at me. "Thank you for coming. The council is waiting for you."

I nodded, grateful I didn't have to speak when he turned and led the way up the expansive stone stairs rising to the building behind us. I might be able to run fearlessly into booby-trap laden tombs and fight off demons, but *this* was scary.

This was a freaking death wish.

On the bright side, at least my sense of self-preservation wasn't totally broken. Some of the crap I'd gotten myself into lately suggested otherwise, so it was a comfort that my danger sensors still worked.

Aidan stuck close by my side as we passed through the large double doors. The interior was more formal than I'd expected, with marble floors and silk wallpaper adorning the large foyer. On one wall, a collection of rare weapons was displayed. *Treasure.* My fingers itched to pocket one. Or ten. They'd look so nice in my trove.

I dragged my gaze away. Stealing from the Alpha Council was not on my to-do list.

My brows rose at the sight of the priceless paintings gracing the other walls. I wasn't much for art, but even I recognized some of these. I didn't know the names, but I didn't need to.

"Are these real?" I asked, stupefied.

Mathias glanced back. "Yes. The Alphas have a taste for the finer things. They've been collecting for years."

"But how are they here? I thought they were in museums." As soon as the words left my mouth, I wanted to curse. *Why* did I have to get curious and basically ask if they'd stolen them?

Idiot.

"You're good at taking things," Mathias said. "So are we."

I swallowed hard. Fears confirmed. The Alpha Council was ruthless and cocky enough to steal the humans' greatest works of art. Supernaturals tried to stay under the radar of humans, but it appeared the Alpha Council was willing to chuck that if they wanted something bad enough. I'd have to keep that in mind.

Mathias led us into a wide hallway. The golden glow from elegant light fixtures gleamed on the wooden floor. Silk wallpaper in a royal purple coated the walls to the wainscoting.

The luxurious surroundings only served to highlight the strangeness of seeing a man being led down the hall, his arms bound in heavy chains, bulky Shifter guards surrounding him, herding him along. His face was downcast, but his magic seethed in the air. I eyed him as he was led past us.

When I thought he was out of earshot, I whispered, "Who the hell was that?"

"A filthy FireSoul the Alpha Council discovered living two villages over. He's being taken to the Prison for Magical Miscreants."

Filthy FireSoul? My stomach dropped and I stutter-stepped. Aidan's hand cupped my arm and pulled me along.

Holy shit. I knew the Alpha Council was vigilant about FireSouls—they didn't want anyone killing off Shifters to steal their shifting power, obviously—but seeing it firsthand was freaking terrifying.

And I'd agreed to come here.

There are lives at stake.

Mathias's words echoed in my head, but they didn't make my heart calm or the sweat dry on my skin.

Mathias led us into a great room that screamed wealth even more loudly than the foyer had. When twelve figures rose from their seats around a massive, gleaming wooden table, I was suddenly immensely grateful for Aidan's presence at my back.

When each Alpha bowed low and murmured their respects, I was even more grateful. Why didn't Aidan sit at this table? Clearly they would accept him here. Besides the two chairs that were clearly meant for us, there was an empty chair, right in the middle on the other side of the table.

Though each Shifter bowed low, their powers still rolled off them in waves that I could smell, taste, and feel. All were different—the scent of warm rain, the taste of meat (gross), the feel of sand beneath my feet, and a dozen others—but all were powerful. They weren't hiding their power, not here in their own stronghold. They wanted anyone who walked into this room to know how powerful they were.

It was easy to see why these were the Alphas. Probably all different species.

When they rose, I got a better look at them. There was a guy who was clearly a lion. He actually looked a lot like Mathias, but with darker hair. A woman with a narrow frame and a graceful sway reminded me of a snake. An enormous man with a dark beard was definitely a bear. I'd bet a hundred dollars—money I didn't have—that he was fond of salmon, especially if he caught it himself. In his mouth while standing in a river.

Upon further examination, I noticed that some people wouldn't look our way. That was odd.

"Thank you for coming." A woman in a simple, medieval-inspired dress stepped forward. Her voice held the sharp crack of authority, and her gaze was cunning. "I am Elenora."

A wolf. No question.

Aidan stepped partially in front of me as if blocking her from getting too close and said, "Good to see you, Elenora. Why don't we sit? It's been a long journey."

Wolf lady nodded, and everyone took their seats. I followed Aidan to the two empty chairs and sat. Thankfully, I was close to a woman who had to be a herbivore. Her large front teeth gave her away.

Not all Shifters looked like the animals they turned into, but it seemed their Alphas all bore a resemblance, probably because they were the strongest of their species and had the most animal magic in them.

I didn't know why Aidan didn't look like a griffin in his human form, but I was grateful. If his nose mimicked his beak, he'd probably fall over from the weight.

"We requested your assistance because we have a problem," Elenora said.

A big one, if they were willing to pay two million dollars to have it fixed. I nodded, hoping she'd continue. Normally, I had no problem speaking up in front of a crowd, but being surrounded by the top members of the Shifters' government made me want to keep as low a profile as possible. If I could sink through this chair and listen from under the table, I would.

I resisted the urge.

Elenora drew in a ragged breath. "Someone has stolen the Heartstone and the Heart of Glencarrough."

Beside me, Aidan flinched.

Uh oh.

"The Heartstone is the protective charm that keeps our stronghold safe," Elenora said. She picked up a small picture that I hadn't noticed lying on the table and passed it down. "That shows the Heartstone."

I squinted at it. It looked like a large sapphire with some kind of carving on it.

"Not only does it conceal the location of Glencarrough, it prevents black magic from being used against the residents," Elenora said. "Without it, this place is no longer hidden from humans. More importantly, if anyone were to attack us, we must fight tooth and claw. While we are partially immune to some magic and can defeat much of what comes for us, we cannot defend against the most grievous magic. There is black magic that could harm us easily."

She stopped, drawing in another shuddering breath, as if to compose herself.

"And the Heart of Glencarrough?" I asked. "What is that?"

"She is a child." Elenora's eyes shined with tears.

My stomach pitched, and a cold sweat broke out on my skin. A child. Stolen from her home.

Like me.

I could remember almost nothing of my past. Only one dark dream of being locked away in a cell with Nix and Del. No parents, no family. Just the three of us. Prisoners, waiting for the Monster to come for us.

"Why did they take her?" I asked.

I held my breath as Elenora composed herself. Everyone at the table looked shaken up, but she was the worst. She was also the leader, from what I could see, and no one stepped in to speak for her. How had she known the girl? Would the child have sat in the empty chair?

"The Heartstone is alive. It looks like a jewel, but it isn't so simple. It is a living force, created from sacrifices made by hundreds of Shifters. It must be tended by the pure of heart. A child is chosen for this task, usually every ten years. Amara is currently the Heart of Glencarrough. Whoever stole the Heartstone knows what it can do, and they know that Amara, or a child like her, is required to keep the Heartstone's magic alive."

Bastards.

"Why do you think they took it?" Aidan asked.

I had my own ideas, and I got the feeling that he did too, but he wanted to hear her say it. So did I.

"To protect something of great value that they own, or to lower our defenses to attack us," Elenora said. "We

45

don't think it was an inside job because all here are loyal, but we have no idea how they got in. It's impossible."

"If it's impossible, it had to be someone from within," I said. "Otherwise the Heartstone would keep them out, right?"

"Theoretically. But no one has gone missing recently. Just Amara."

"What about not recently?"

"Well, there are some, of course. Not everyone wants to live at the stronghold forever, and there are reasons to leave." Her gaze darted to Aidan, then away.

Strange.

But I could easily see why people would leave here. Despite its beauty, it was an intimidating place. Cold and formal. And it didn't matter if it'd been a Shifter who'd stolen Amara. I wasn't looking for clues the old-fashioned way. I'd follow my dragon sense and face whatever was on the other side.

"Will you take the job?" Elenora asked.

The immediate self-preservation part of me wanted to say no, of course. But this was a child. An innocent stolen away from her home.

Like I had been.

"Yes. I'll start right—"

The door crashed open behind me, the sound cracking through the room. The rabbit Shifter next to me flinched. Annoyance and concern flashed over the faces of the others.

"You convened a meeting without me?" A deep voice bellowed from behind. Rage and pain echoed in the sound. "My daughter is missing, and I don't even get my seat at the table?"

Elenora rose, reaching a hand out. "You're distraught, Angus."

I turned to see a huge man charging toward me. His eyes were sharp and his muscles bulging. He was some kind of predator Shifter. A powerful one. If I had to bet, his was the empty seat across from me, not Amara's.

His strides ate up the ground, and he crowded in front of me, looking like he wanted to wrap his hands around my throat. I reached for my knife.

"So, you think you can find my daughter? A Magica scum?" Insane grief glinted in his eyes and echoed in his voice. His breath, which smelled like he hadn't brushed his teeth in a week, wafted over my face. His gaze darted to Aidan. "A Magica who allies with the Origin?"

I almost flinched at the disgust in his voice. Instinct made me want to slip my dagger between his ribs, but no way in hell could I do that in front of the Alpha Council. And I wasn't a big enough bitch to stab someone's dad, even if they didn't like my kind.

Aidan surged between us, pushing the man back. They were the same height and weight, but the threat and power radiating from Aidan made him appear bigger.

"Watch it, Angus." Aidan's voice was low with warning. Even I shivered. "I can ignore your problem with me, but I won't let you treat Cass that way."

Problem with Aidan? There was a history here.

Angus's gaze darted to mine. "Your magic smells strange, girl. Something off there."

Fear pitched my stomach. I wasn't using my magic! He shouldn't be able to smell me. Could he smell the FireSoul in me now that I'd started to use my power more? Did it linger?

"You sure you don't use black magic?" Angus demanded. "How can we trust you'll find Amara? That you aren't on the side of whoever took her? You're on the side of the Origin, after all."

Aidan grabbed Angus's arm and spun him toward the door. "That's enough. Cass is here to help. I don't care if Amara's your daughter, you'll respect Cass."

Elenora hurried to Angus's side and grabbed his other arm. Together, Elenora and Aidan dragged him to the door. Elenora was stronger than she looked, but Angus wasn't going quietly. He kept turning around to glare at me, spitting insults.

My heart pounded in my throat as I watched. Were these other Shifters sniffing the air now, trying to catch a whiff of my strange magic?

I'd known I was going from the frying pan into the fire when I'd come here, but this was worse than I'd expected. I wanted to turn around and blurt that I was a Mirror Mage. That I'd just borrowed another's powers and that was why I smelled strange. It wasn't me!

But that'd make me look desperate and even more suspicious, which I really didn't need.

I couldn't help but take a quick glance over my shoulder. The gazes of the eleven people standing around the table were split between me, Aidan, and Elenora. The gazes that landed on me glinted with suspicion.

I swallowed hard and turned back around, my skin chilled. It was unlikely they suspected what I actually was—at least I prayed so—but Shifters were notoriously suspicious of Magica. If one of their kind pointed the finger at me, they'd be sure to look twice.

Aidan and Elenora thrust Angus out of the room. Elenora leaned out and told Angus to get some rest, her voice sharp, then shut the door. She turned and followed Aidan back toward me. I tried to keep my face impassive as they approached.

"Thank you for agreeing to do this," Elenora said. Her nose twitched as if she were sniffing the air.

My heart threatened to break my ribs. "I could hardly say no once you told me it was a little girl."

"I assume you need something of hers?" Elenora asked as she reached into a pocket of her flowing skirt. "To track her, I mean."

She pulled a ragged plush rabbit out of her pocket. My heart almost snapped in two when I saw the thin little bunny, its cotton fur worn off in places and its plastic eyes dull.

I tried to keep my hand from trembling as I reached out to take it, but I didn't actually need it to track Amara in the way Elenora thought I did. I just couldn't help but touch it.

My dragon sense was based on covetousness. Dragons coveted and could find treasure. Treasure could be anything or anyone of value. The people in this room valued Amara so much that I could just latch my magic onto that. But knowing a few key facts about what I was hunting didn't hurt, and just knowing that the little girl loved a rabbit like this was enough.

The connection came to me naturally, a vague pull toward her location. Not far. Only a couple hours perhaps. We could be there by nightfall.

"I'll take this with me, if that's okay," I said. I wanted to give it to her if—when—I found her.

Elenora nodded. "All right. Do you need anything else? Can we send people with you to help?"

"Not now. If I need help, I'll ask." I couldn't afford to be near any more Shifters. If I needed help, I'd ask my *deirfiúr.* And that was unlikely. "Nine times out of ten, these jobs require stealth rather than force. And if I need force, I have the Origin."

Elenora's eyes flared with appreciation. "That you do. Mathias will be your contact. He'll get you anything you need."

"Okay. We'll go now. I want to get started." And I wanted to get the heck out of this room.

I glanced at Aidan and he nodded, his dark gaze solemn.

"We'll be in touch if we need anything else," he said.

I could feel a dozen sets of eyes on my back as I followed him out of the room. My neck burned, a sick twist of fear in my stomach. I'd gotten complacent in my life back in Magic's Bend, only surrounding myself with a few people I could trust. Coming here reminded me that there was a whole world of supernaturals out there who might figure out what I was.

And if that happened, I'd probably wish I were dead.

CHAPTER FOUR

We stepped out into the hall to find Mathias waiting for us. I was grateful to see that Angus wasn't with him, though I wished Mathias hadn't been there at all. From his *filthy FireSoul* comment, he was clearly as biased as the rest of them against my kind.

When Mathias's nose twitched as if he was smelling the air, I tensed. Confusion creased his brow.

Damn it. Angus must have said something to him, and now he thought my magic smelled odd as well.

I wanted both to distract him and get away from him. "The girl isn't very far away. Perhaps a couple of hours. It's remote out here. Will you get us some food to take? Maybe a blanket for her when we find her and any other things she might want? Like her jacket. It'll comfort her, and she'll know her family sent us."

He nodded. "Absolutely. I'll meet you at the car."

"Thank you." My tension didn't decrease as he turned and walked away. I couldn't get out of here fast enough.

Aidan and I hurried down the hall.

"That was smart," he said.

"Thanks."

My skin pricked as we walked through the Alpha Council's stronghold. Where was that FireSoul now? Was he still chained up? In a dungeon somewhere? A cold sweat broke out on my skin.

That could be me. My *deirfiúr*.

When we pushed out through the great front doors, I sucked in a breath of fresh air. It didn't do much to make me feel better. Getting far beyond Glencarrough's gates was the only thing that would shake this fear from me.

We walked down the stairs and leaned against the car to wait. It seemed that Aidan and I had come to an unspoken agreement that now was not the time to chat. I tried to focus on the sound of the birds, the cool breeze, anything other than my location and the fact that Shifters kept looking my way.

Screw this.

I climbed into the car. Aidan could say goodbye to Mathias. I needed to close myself off from these Shifters.

Matthias joined us ten minutes later, his arms laden with bags and a cooler. He handed them off to Aidan, who loaded them into the trunk.

Mathias loomed outside the car door, so I opened it. There was a fine line between protecting myself from Shifters sensing my magic and hiding out like a hermit.

"Thanks for the stuff," I said, itching to get out of here.

"Thank you for doing this," Matthias said.

"Can't say no to a missing kid."

He nodded and I shut the door. Through the window, I watched Aidan shake Matthias's hand. Then he climbed in and cranked the engine.

Aidan didn't speak as we drove out of the compound and through the gate. My shoulders were tensely bunched muscles until we were a few hundred yards away. Even then, relaxation didn't come easily.

"You know where she is?" Aidan finally asked.

"Yes. Fairly close. Within two hours. Somewhere in the mountains north of here. I'm close enough that I should be getting a more localized feeling of where she is, but it's scattered."

"Magic?"

"Probably. This girl sounds like she's valuable. Not to mention the Heartstone. Whoever stole her is going to be taking precautions. Let's get closer and I should get a better feel for it." At least, that's how it normally worked. It wasn't an exact science, that was for sure. Just intuition. A feeling that was never wrong.

We drove in silence, the desolate mountains rolling past. My stomach churned at the thought of how Amara must feel. I didn't have specific memories of my childhood—just the one nightmare I'd had last week. But it wasn't a stretch to think that Amara might be locked up in a dungeon like I had been.

"Why aren't you on the Alpha Council?" I asked when thinking about Amara became too much. "You were clearly the most powerful one there."

"Yeah, but that's part of the problem. The Alpha Council is about equality. They make decisions together.

Elenora leads formal sessions, but she's not in charge. I'd create unbalance."

There was something in his voice that I couldn't pinpoint, but it definitely sounded off. "Yeah, I guess I can see that. But you don't want to be on it?"

"Not really." His fists tightened on the wheel, knuckles standing out white. "I like my life, and I've got enough responsibility with Origin Enterprises. And trust me—they don't want me there."

"There's something you're not telling me." I could hear it in his voice. There was a darkness to it when he talked about not being wanted. And the way Angus had spoken about him…

"And there's plenty you haven't told me."

That shut me up fast. He was right. Hadn't he said it earlier? We all had secrets. Bad stuff about us, as he'd put it. Was his estrangement from the Alpha Council one of his?

My dragon sense pulled hard then. We were close.

I pointed to a turn in the road. "Turn there."

Aidan turned the Range Rover onto the gravel road. A sheep scampered out of the way, charging up the mountain on the left. The sun was beginning to set, sending orange light over the hills and valleys.

"We're close. I can feel it." I reached down and ran my hand over the knife at my thigh.

"Magic, Cass," Aidan said.

"I can use both." I squinted ahead, looking for something out of the ordinary. The desolate peaks and valleys of the Highlands stretched out before me, cut through by the tiny gravel road we traveled.

"What the hell is that?" Aidan asked, pointing ahead of us about a hundred yards.

The structure was so well hidden that it took me a while to find it. Not only did the brown stone wall blend in with the mountain behind it, but magic had been used to help conceal it. A human would never have noticed it.

The structure was built into the mountainside, using the mountain itself for walls and part of the roof. But the distinctive domed top protruded just enough to make my heart sink.

"Shit," I said. "Stop the car."

Aidan pulled to a halt.

"That's it ahead, but we need to approach on foot," I said. We were about as close as we were going to get in the car anyway. "I have a feeling this is going to be a problem."

"Her abductor didn't take her far."

"No. He must not have a transport charm." I used them occasionally, but they were damned hard to come by. "And even if they did, this is a good place to hide out. If it's what I think it is, it's very protected."

I climbed out of the car. Sharp wind cut through my leather jacket. I shivered. Even in summer, the Highlands were chilly. And night was falling. Sunset would come any second now.

We made our way silently up the mountain, careful not to let rocks slide beneath our feet. When I neared the flat wall that protruded from the mountainside, the electric zip of protective magic streaked across my skin. It prickled uncomfortably, warning me away.

"Strong magic," Aidan muttered.

"Yeah," I whispered. "The ancients who built this were good with protective spells."

My gaze roved over the stone wall. I could see no door or hidden entry. Just a flat expanse of stone blocks. I skirted around it and gestured to Aidan to follow me. I scrambled up the last bit of the mountain toward the dome at the top, trying to keep my footing on the steepest bit.

I reached the edge of the dome. Because we were standing above the main part of the temple, the magic was even stronger here. Tiny electric shocks skittered all over my skin. If we screwed with this kind of magic or tried to break in, the protective spells would put up a hell of a fight. Might even collapse the temple, sealing in its contents.

And Amara.

Damn, it was getting dark. I glanced back over my shoulder to see that the sun had disappeared beneath the mountains. We needed to make this quick.

I turned back to the dome. There was enough light to see that the great stone blocks were fitted carefully together to form the gracefully curved shape, a feat of ancient engineering that impressed even me. Stone blocks of a darker shade of brown spelled out *Camhanaich.*

Dawn in ancient Scots Gaelic. I couldn't speak the language, but I'd raided two Dawn Temples before, so I recognized the shape of the word even if I couldn't speak the language.

Disappointment pierced me, sharp and bitter, and my shoulders sagged.

I wanted to stomp my feet and scream my frustration to the night, but I didn't want to alert whoever was inside the temple. They probably wouldn't hear me through all the rock, but better safe than sorry.

"We gotta get out of here," I whispered. "Back to the car."

"We can't just leave her."

My heart twisted at the idea of the little girl trapped in the temple. "I know, damn it. Just trust me for now."

We made our way down the mountain, careful to keep our steps quiet. When we slipped back into the car, Aidan turned to me.

"What the hell was that?" he asked.

"*That* was a Dawn Temple."

"A what?"

"It's locked until dawn. And I mean *locked*. Those enchantments are serious. I didn't want whoever was in there to hear us talking, though it was unlikely."

"What's a Dawn Temple?"

"They were built thousands of years ago by a group of Magica who worshipped the sun. You know how human archaeological sites like the Mayan pyramids are built to allow the sun's rays into a special chamber at the solstice?"

"Yeah. This does that too?"

"Worse. These temples were built as places of worship. Like many religions, they had holy relics they wanted to protect. I've raided a couple. They took a page out of the humans' book—or vise versa, I don't know—and made it so that these temples will use the sun's rays to trigger a spell that lowers the protection spells at dawn so that it can be entered."

I pointed to the flat stone wall we'd passed that had looked like it had no door. "That's the entrance. It's the only part of the temple that's not made of mountain, besides the dome at the top. We'll still have to figure out how exactly to get in because I don't see a normal door, but at least we'll have a shot once the protections are lowered."'"

He nodded. "And the dome is the part that catches the sun's light. That's why it says 'Dawn.' It triggers a spell."

"Yep. You speak Scots Gaelic?"

"Yes."

"Talented."

"You have no idea."

"And cocky."

"It's not cocky if it's true." His grave gaze turned back to the temple. "So you're saying we can't get in until dawn."

"Right. It's impenetrable. The protective spells are too strong."

"I felt that. I might be able to blow through the top. Or move the rock somehow."

"Possibly, but whoever built this took Elemental Mages into account. Even if you could get in, it wouldn't be without a big mess. It'd alert whoever is inside. If they have a transport charm, they could run with Amara. Or hurt her."

"Agreed. The risk is too great. They don't want to kill her because they need her. So we'll come back tomorrow at dawn and sneak in."

"Yeah. We'll still have to figure out how to get in, but the worst of the protective magic should be dropped."

"Once we're in, we won't be able to get out until the next dawn, right?"

"Depends on the spell. Most of the time, they just wanted to keep people out. We won't know until we get in if we're going to have to wait till the next dawn to leave."

"We'll deal with it then. In the meantime, we need to find a place to stay the night. Close enough that it's easy to get back here early."

"I'm not going back to Glencarrough." I shivered. We hadn't driven past any towns between here and the stronghold, but no way I'd go back there. We'd have to find something. "What's near here?"

His shoulders tightened and his knuckles turned white where he gripped the wheel. I could almost feel his tension.

He sighed. "I know a place nearby. No one will bother us there."

He started the engine, then did a three-point turn on the little road.

"But you don't want to go there," I said. "Why?"

"Not particularly, but it's safe and close. That's more than we can say for anything else around here. It'd be stupid not to take advantage."

I frowned when he didn't answer the *why* in my question, but dropped it. "Okay."

About thirty minutes later, Aidan pulled the Range Rover onto an even smaller gravel road. A sharp zing of protective spells zipped through me, like a thousand pricks of a pin. I wanted to turn back immediately, which was no doubt the purpose of the spell.

"Ouch. You weren't kidding about this place being protected." The way the magic pricked against my skin was enough warning to stay away.

I glanced at him. His brow was furrowed and his fists gripped around the wheel. "You feel it too? Aren't they your protection spells?"

If so, he should be exempt. Like how I could enter Ancient Magic when it was locked up, but other people couldn't.

"They aren't my spells," he said. "They're old. About twenty years. But they were made to allow me to enter. If they weren't, they'd have knocked me and you on our asses about a hundred yards ago. They're just so strong that they even affect people who are allowed to be here. It'll pass."

Weird. I'd never heard of protection spells that strong. From what I could feel, it was like an invisible force field that repelled anyone who wasn't Aidan or his invited guest. That took a *lot* of magic. Considering how swank his place in Ireland was, I couldn't wait to see this place. Must be a castle.

The car slowed as we reached a collection of small buildings. Though it was dark, the moon was full enough that I could make out the stone structures with thatched roofs. They were tiny and run down. When Aidan pulled the car to a halt in front of the largest building and got out, I frowned.

This was the place those badass protection spells were guarding? It was a hovel compared to his house in Ireland. It was a hovel compared to pretty much any house. Whoever had owned this place didn't have a lot of money, so why had they spent such a massive amount on protection spells? Spells this strong usually took a few Magica to create. They'd be pricey.

Aidan got out of the car and I followed.

The chill night air hit me. I wrapped my arms around myself. "What is this place?"

Aidan grabbed the bags from the trunk and headed toward the front door.

"Aidan? Did you hear me?" I ran to catch up.

"Yeah." His voice was gruff. "Sorry, mind wandered. It's just a place I own."

He stepped onto the stoop and ran his hand along the perimeter of the wooden door, no doubt unlocking another protection spell. When he removed his hand, some of the prickling on my skin dissipated, like the spell had deactivated. It was now almost comfortable to be here.

Almost.

Aidan pushed open the heavy wooden door and stepped over the threshold. He waved a hand and a few lanterns burst into flame, sending a dim glow around the small cottage.

"Being an Elemental Mage sure is handy," I said absently as I took in the room.

He grunted and walked to the rustic kitchen in the corner and put the bags on the small counter. I couldn't see a microwave or anything modern like that, but there was an ancient fridge, and the rest of the space was equally old-fashioned. There was a tiny living room with no TV and a dining nook with a sturdy oak table.

"So this isn't your hunting lodge?" I asked. It was the only thing I could think of for a place as remote as this, but I couldn't imagine a guy like Aidan here. He was rich as hell and this place wasn't charming rustic. It was just rustic rustic.

Added to that, he really didn't seem happy to be here. His shoulders were tense, and he wasn't usually so silent. Worse, his magic felt more chaotic, like he had less control of it. The sound of crashing ocean waves that I usually associated with his magic but didn't often hear was thunderous. And his magic's forest scent was stronger than ever, like a rainstorm had stirred up the evergreen.

"No," he said. "I'm going to go get some firewood."

Bemused, I watched him stomp out the door.

Very weird.

I touched the silver charm at my neck, using my magic to ignite its spell. I had a cellphone, but international fees were a bitch, so I preferred using my comms charm to get in touch with my *deirfiúr* when on jobs.

"Nix?" I said. "Del?"

There was a crackle and rustle, then Del's voice came through. "Hey! How's it going? What's the job? Are we rich yet?"

I almost laughed, but the thought of Amara crushed it.

"Cass? Del?" Nix's voice came through clearly.

"Hi, Nix," I said as I walked to the sunken couch and sat.

"Hey. How are you? Are you being safe?"

"Yes."

"What's the job?" Del asked.

"Is it dangerous?" Nix added.

My voice caught in my throat. "It's a little girl named Amara. She was stolen from the Alpha Council stronghold."

There was silence at the other end.

"Shiiit," Del finally breathed.

"That sucks."

I told them all about the Heartstone and Amara's role in tending it. "And I've found her. I just can't get to her until tomorrow morning when the protections around the Dawn Temple drop."

"Damn. But at least they need her alive so that she can tend the stone, right?" Nix asked.

"Yeah." It was the only thought keeping me going, honestly.

"Where are you now?" Del asked.

"Some weird, ramshackle cabin that Aidan owns. But it's surrounded by more protection spells than even his estate in Ireland. But it's a dump. It totally doesn't fit with his lifestyle of private planes and estates. Honestly, it's more our speed."

Until we'd settled in Magic's Bend and started making some decent money off of Ancient Magic, we'd stayed in a lot of places like this. Hell, this was nice compared to the barns and abandoned shacks we'd lived in our first couple years on the run.

I glanced down at the little wooden table next to the couch. My eye caught on a carving. I leaned closer.

Aidan.

The name was scratched in awkwardly, as if by a child.

"Holy shit," I breathed.

"What?" Nix demanded.

"His name is scratched into the table. I think he grew up here."

"Weird. So he didn't come from money."

"No. He made it himself. He told me that much before. But he never mentioned he grew up like this." The prickle of the protection spells that affected even him popped into my mind. "It's not the poverty. It's the protection spells I'm weirded out by."

"Yeah, that's strange," Nix said. "Ask him about it."

"Yeah, I will."

"By the way," Del said. "That scroll is still sitting in your trove, right? Along with the Chalice of Youth."

"Yeah." I knew I needed to find a safe place for the two dangerous items I'd recovered on the job I'd done with Aidan last week. "But if he gets the scroll, he can read it and find out that you and Nix are FireSouls as well."

It was one of the big reasons I didn't want to give it to him.

"I know," Del said. "But if we trust him with your life, we trust him with ours. You know he's the best person to take care of the scroll. He could lock them up in some super vault he probably has."

True. It was literally Aidan's job to protect stuff. But still, Del was always the least wary of us.

"I don't know, Del. Your life is more valuable to me than my own. And Nix's. I've got a lot to lose here, so I'm wary. There's so much I don't know about him. He's too good to be true, right?"

"That house doesn't sound too good to be true," Nix said. "Talk to him some more. Learn about him."

"I actually like that his origins are closer to ours. It's the protection spells that bother me. Whoever lived here was poor. If they put so much money into buying these spells… That says nothing good."

"Ask him about it," Nix demanded. "Seriously. Not just for your own curiosity. We need a place to store that damn scroll and the Chalice of Youth. It's dangerous having it in your trove. If you trust him, I trust him."

"Okay, okay. I will," I said. "Look, I've got to go. I'll get in touch with you soon."

"Thanks for checking in," Nix said.

"Yeah. And good luck with the kid."

"Thanks, Del. Talk to you guys later." I pressed my fingers to the charm again and the connection broke.

I couldn't help but run my fingers over the *Aidan* carved into the table before I stood and went to the little kitchen. What had his childhood been like, living in this place?

There was too much I didn't know about him. Maybe if I fed him, he'd be more inclined to talk.

I sorted through the bags on the counter, putting the one full of Amara's clothes to the side and digging some chips out of one of the canvas bags full of snacks. I peered into the cooler and found a dozen big sandwiches and tiny foil packets of mustard and mayo. I silently thanked Matthias and the Alpha Council for being so well-prepared. There was enough here to eat and still have plenty left over for tomorrow when we got Amara.

I dug out a few sandwiches and some drinks—cans of the Scottish soda Irn Bru—then grabbed the chips and carried them to the table. I was setting them down as Aidan entered, his arms full of freshly split wood.

He kicked the door shut behind him and carried the wood over to the fire.

"You're pretty good with an axe," I said as I watched him lay the pale wood in the fire.

"Had some practice," he said as he waved his hand at the wood. It burst into flame.

"Why did you need to get the wood? Can't you just make fire?"

"Yeah, but it's easier if there's something to burn. This way, I can just ignore it once it's lit." He shook out his arms, as if an uncomfortable chill had raced over them.

It was weird to see him out of sorts. Normally, he was so relaxed and in control of a situation. But this place had him on edge.

"I got us some dinner," I said, gesturing to the food on the table.

"Thanks." He took the chair next to me. Up close, there were shadows in his eyes.

I unwrapped my sandwich and bit in, giving Aidan a chance to get some food in him before I interrogated him. I sure as hell wouldn't answer painful questions if I was hungry, so wouldn't he be the same?

Also, I didn't like talking about difficult stuff. I had enough bad shit in my past that I liked to focus on the good.

I swallowed the last bite of my sandwich. "So, did you grow up here?"

Aidan's gaze met mine and he stopped chewing. After a second, he swallowed and said, "Why do you ask?"

"Your name is carved into that little end table over there."

"Yeah. I did."

"That's cool."

He glanced around at the place. "Not really."

"This place is fine," I said. "You should see some of the places Del, Nix, and I have lived. Yikes."

"Yeah, but none of them were locked down like Fort Knox. Even I can feel the prickle of the spells."

I winced. This was the tricky part. "That's true. So, uh, why all the protection spells? I haven't felt anything like this before. Not even in tombs filled with tons of gold. I mean, unless you've got some treasure locked away in those other buildings, it seems pretty intense."

And by intense, I meant utterly nuts. It was like the human equivalent of building six lava-filled moats around a shack in the woods. And I could feel that there was no treasure. My dragon sense usually picked up on that kind of thing.

"Intense is one way to put it. And those other buildings are just a workshop and a piecemeal gym. There's no treasure, so don't get any ideas." Despite the shadows in his eyes, his mouth tugged up at the corner.

"Har har."

"You really don't know why this place is like this?" he asked.

"No. Should I?"

He shrugged. "You're not a Shifter, so I guess not."

"It's Shifter business? Wait. Does our proximity to Glencarrough have anything to do with this?"

We'd actually driven partway back to Glencarrough to get here. From my limited understanding of the geography, Glencarrough was the closest settlement to this place.

He nodded, staring at his hands, then flexed his palm and clenched it into a fist. "You asked why I wasn't on the Alpha Council. And you're right—it's odd that the Origin isn't on the Alpha Council."

I nodded, urging him to continue. The way the Alpha Council ran their business was a bit of a mystery to non-Shifters. Magica and Shifters didn't usually hang out much. We certainly didn't talk about the structure of our governments.

"For centuries, we were on the Council," Aidan said. "Until my father. I actually lived with him until I was fourteen."

"I thought you said he died when you were young and that your mom raised you."

"Fourteen feels young now. And I don't like to talk about him, so I say that. I found my mother after he died and she raised me from fourteen to eighteen. She's the only one I want to remember."

"Why?"

"When I was twelve, my father had a disagreement with two other council members. They couldn't come to terms on some council business. Something fairly minor, though I never learned what exactly." He dragged a hand through his hair, clearly uncomfortable. "He killed them."

"Holy shit," I breathed. "Why?"

"That's only part of the ugly part." He reached across the table and picked up my hand. His fingers were warm and strong. He turned my hand over and looked down at my palm, as if he were reading my fortune.

After a second, I realized that he didn't want to look at me, though he did want a connection. My fingers curled around his.

His voice was gruff when he finally spoke. "Some Origins have been known to have rage issues. Scholars of magic think it's all the built-up power and the fighting spirits of the animals we can become. Not every origin is hit with it, but some are. My father was one of them. One day, he snapped. For the first time in Alpha Council history, there was murder. After he killed the two other council members, he holed up here and put all the protections in place. It was his family's land—I'd spent some time here as a little kid—but we moved here full time after the murder. He never left this land, and no one could get to him. The Alpha Council decided to pardon him. Or at least, not seek vengeance. He was too powerful and too protected. Some people are still angry about that decision. Like Angus."

"Yeah, he didn't seem to like you today."

"No. Because I went with my father. I was old enough to know better, but I stuck by him."

"You were a kid. You were freaking twelve! Of course you stuck by him."

"Twelve is old enough to know better. He was a murderer who used his power to avoid punishment. But he was my father. I didn't want to believe he was evil and I couldn't leave him. I became a traitor to the other Shifters when I went with him."

"Because you didn't want to betray your father. There was no winning for you."

He shrugged.

"So you grew up here? With him?"

"Yeah. It, uh, wasn't an easy childhood, even before he killed his fellow council members." His gaze met mine, strong and fearless.

I couldn't really imagine what it must have been like to live on this secluded piece of land with a guy whose insanity manifested itself as rage, but I had a feeling that might only be because I couldn't remember my past.

"You turned out good though." I squeezed his hand.

"Thanks. And it's done with, so it doesn't matter. After he died, I found my mother. He'd told me she was dead, but I found some of her things in his room. She took care of me. Turned me into a decent man. Eventually, I approached the council to make amends for going with my father that day."

"And they forgave you, obviously, because you were just a kid." I hated that he was so hard on himself.

"Yeah, most of them. A few, like Angus, can't recover from the loss of the men my father killed, so they hate me. I don't blame them. Because of that, I thought it best that I not sit on the council. I don't think the family curse is going to get me—most Origins go mad by their early twenties—but the Council needs some distance from me."

"I guess." I glanced around the room.

"Thanks for dinner." His tone indicated the conversation was done. Sharing was one thing, but dealing with the aftermath was another. "I'm going to head out to the gym and beat up a punching bag for an hour. There's two bedrooms. Take the one with the bigger bed." He turned and strode to the door.

"Uh, thanks," I said to his retreating back. I couldn't blame him for bailing out. It was how I liked to handle emotional shit too.

When the door shut behind him, I went to the little window over the kitchen counter and looked out. Aidan's big strides ate up the ground as he headed toward the small building about twenty yards away.

I turned around and scrubbed my hands through my hair, trying to get a grip on the emotions ricocheting through me. While I hated that Aidan's life had been so shitty when he was a kid, the way he'd risen above it only made me respect him more.

And trust him more, too.

Oh, boy. I was in trouble.

CHAPTER FIVE

Cold, damp stone bit into my back as I huddled against the wall. My heart pounded, a terrified drumbeat in my head. Footsteps sounded in the hall outside our dungeon cell.

I squeezed myself into a ball, trying to disappear into the stone. If I could just make myself small enough, he wouldn't find me. I didn't know where they took the girls when they left this dark little hole, but they came back different.

Collared.

The door crashed open and light blinded me. It pounded into my head. I hadn't seen light in days. I scrambled back, my shoulder bumping against the girl next to me. Instinctively, I flinched. But when she grabbed on to me, I latched on to her right back. Like my muscles remembered that we were friends even if my mind was too scared to remember.

The figure that stood silhouetted in the door was huge. A monster. I bit my tongue to keep from screaming. Anything to keep from drawing attention to myself.

"In you go." His voice sounded like rocks scraping together.

His arm moved and a small figure hurtled into the room. I hadn't seen the girl standing in front of him, but he'd shoved her.

Gratitude welled inside me when I realized he wasn't coming for one of us. But when he slammed the door and the girl started to cry, shame washed over me. The only reason he wasn't taking one of us was that he already had.

And now she was back.

I sucked in a deep breath and scrambled forward. Even though we were alone in the room—me and the other girls—I still moved low to the ground, with stealth. It was instinct.

When I reached the girl, I pulled her up by her arms. Though I couldn't see in the dark, there were other arms as well. My friends. We picked up the girl and half-dragged/half-carried her back into the corner with us. When we reached it, we huddled into a pile.

Tears rolled down my cheeks. Was this my life?

I hugged the girl nearest me, not sure who it was because of the dark. When I felt the cold metal around her neck, I realized. It was the girl who'd been tossed back in the room.

She now wore a collar.

I bolted upright in bed, gasping. The dark closed in on me, suffocating and blinding. I blinked frantically, trying to make out anything in the cloying blackness. The quilt beneath my fingertips was soft cotton, not stone.

I wasn't there anymore.

I was in Scotland. In Aidan's childhood home.

Safe.

No longer a prisoner or trapped in my own nightmares. I sank my fingers into the quilt, trying to anchor myself to the real world. My heaving breaths were loud in the silence.

This dream had been new, but had felt like a continuation of the one I'd had over a week ago. I was finally remembering my past, but the things I was dredging up...

Freaking awful.

I dragged a shaky hand through my hair and rubbed my eyes. I had to get out of this room. I couldn't risk falling back asleep like this. Not if it meant having that horrible nightmare again. And as much as I wanted to understand my past, I clearly needed to experience it in small doses.

With a trembling hand, I reached for my lightstone ring on the bedside table. The glow burst to life when I put it on. Soft light illuminated the small room. I'd gone to bed before Aidan had come back, but before I'd fallen asleep, I'd heard him come in and go into the other bedroom.

The last thing I needed was a chat, though.

As quietly as I could, I climbed out of bed and tugged on my jeans and boots, then zipped myself into my jacket. I strapped my daggers to my thighs, then tiptoed through the living room and out the front door.

The night was damp and cool, and I sucked in the cold air, hoping to clear my head as I walked silently across the grass toward the building that Aidan had gone to earlier in the night.

Though I had nervous energy to burn after that nightmare, I'd be fooling myself if I said that was the only reason I was going to the gym. It was where Aidan had escaped last night when he'd felt uncomfortable. Uncomfortable was an understatement for how I felt right now, but maybe it would work for me too. And maybe it'd tell me more about Aidan.

Yeah, it was a bad idea to get involved, but the more I learned about him, the more I wanted to know. And right now, I'd rather try to think about a guy than my past.

The heavy wooden door creaked as I pushed it open. My lightstone illuminated the small space as I stepped inside. A few pieces of ramshackle exercise equipment—weight benches, punching bags of various sizes, pull-up bars—decorated the space, but that was about it.

Had Aidan worked out when he was young to keep himself strong, so he could withstand his father's rage episodes? I shuddered at the thought, my heart twisting in my chest at the idea of a small Aidan being subject to that kind of abuse. He'd been stuck here for most of his childhood, living with a monster.

I was proof that you could survive it, but I hated the idea of anyone I cared for going through something similar.

I dragged my jacket off and hung it on a hook by the door, then went to the punching bag in the corner. It was the big, bulky kind. Roughly the size of a man if you chopped him off at the knees. I wanted to do that to Aidan's father. To the Monster who'd stolen my memories. To the one who'd captured Amara.

I launched my fist at the leather bag. *Smack!* The force of the hit jolted up my arm. I didn't usually work out—my job kept me too busy—but pulverizing an inanimate object felt good. My fists flew, pounding into the bag. The lightstone ring on my hand flashed with every blow, the effect almost hypnotizing.

My breathing started to drag, my lungs burning. After a while, I realized that tears rolled down my cheeks, but I didn't stop to wipe them away. I just kept hitting, wailing on the bag like I wanted to wail on so many bad guys that I couldn't catch because they were hiding or locked up in a damned Dawn Temple or already dead.

Eventually, a shadow caught my eye. My muscles tensed, ready to turn on any attack. But it was Aidan.

Of course. He was the only one who could get in here, anyway. The protection spells were too strong.

He didn't say anything, just leaned against the wall. I hit the punching bag a few more times, but the fight had drained out of me. I sniffled and dragged my sleeve across my cheeks.

"Can't sleep?" I asked, trying to sound normal.

"Not once I heard you get up."

"How long have you been here?"

He approached, seeming to have waited until I was done beating the crap out of the bag.

"Long enough," he said, then pulled me into his arms.

I stiffened, but his warmth enveloped me. My face pressed against the soft flannel covering his hard chest. Fates, he felt good.

"Are you trying to comfort me?" I mumbled into his shirt. I couldn't smell his magic right now, but I could smell him. Soap and skin and Aidan. I wanted to breathe him in forever.

"Yeah, maybe." His big hand rested on the back of my head, stroking my hair, and his other wrapped around my waist. "Am I doing it right?"

I nodded, sniffling. The tears were past, thank magic, but I didn't want to let go.

"What was that all about?" he asked after a moment.

"Just felt like a workout."

"Oh, yeah. Right. Those midnight workouts that involve crying. Those really make me feel the burn. I alternate them with leg days."

I laughed, the sound muffled against his shirt. Now that the crying had stopped, I had a chance to focus on how good Aidan felt.

And damn, did he feel good. He towered over me, seeming tall and strong as a mountain. Heat coiled within me. I tried to ignore it.

"But really. What's wrong?"

I dragged in a ragged breath. "I guess this job just hits close to home. I can't stop thinking about Amara."

Or my past. Or your past. Why was the world so damned cruel?

"Close to home? You told me about the Monster who hunts you, but not about how you met him. I know almost nothing about your past."

The nightmare flashed in my mind. *That* was my past. Why would I want to tell anyone that?

I squeezed my eyes shut, trying to banish the feeling of the dark stone cell. I didn't want to think about my past, not now that I was feeling a bit better. Being held like this made me remember the good things there were in life, not just my ugly past or Amara.

I sunk my fingers into Aidan's shirt, wanting to grab hold of his strength and use it to force the bad memories away.

"Nothing interesting in my past," I said.

"Now, I know that's not true. I showed you mine, so you ought to show me yours."

I laughed. He was talking about revealing dark pasts, but my mind went straight toward what it might be like if he *showed me his*.

That was a better way to forget this misery for a while.

I ran my hand up his chest, reveling in the hard muscles beneath my palms. I raised my head to meet his gaze.

Fates, he was handsome, especially when the concern in his gray eyes turned to heat as he registered my intentions.

"Cass." Aidan's voice was rough.

His hand tightened in my hair, and heat flared low in my belly. I stood on tiptoe and pulled hard at his shirt, dragging him down until I could crush my mouth against his.

His lips were warm and soft, a contrast to the hard body that pressed against my own. I wanted to climb him like a tree.

The low groan that escaped his throat spiked my desire higher. Ravenous, I ran my hands over his shoulders and chest, wanting nothing more than to rip his shirt off and kiss every inch of him.

His mouth felt like heaven on mine. When his tongue traced the seam of my lips, I parted them. He slipped between my lips, and my brain fogged. Every bad thought was drifting away as pleasure swamped me.

I pressed myself closer to him, gasping at the skill of his kiss and his hardness against my belly. Need flooded me, a desire like I'd never felt. This wasn't just any guy.

This was Aidan. I didn't care that he was a millionaire and the most powerful Shifter in the world. He'd had my back every time something bad had come at me. He'd had no reason to come on this job except to be by my side.

Then the thought of the job—of Amara—stole my breath.

I jerked away, gasping.

"What's wrong?" Aidan's voice was strained. The desire in his dark eyes was fierce. I shivered.

"Nothing," I said as I pulled away. "At least, not with you. But I can't stop thinking about Amara. We can't fail her."

"We won't."

"I want to practice shifting again." I *needed* to practice. I couldn't keep running from my magic, not when bigger things were at stake than me lying low from the Order of the Magica or the Alpha Council. "I've got a better handle on the lightning and my Mirror Mage powers, but shifting is still so damned hard. What if I need it to save her?"

Approval gleamed in his eyes. He'd been pushing me to practice and embrace my magic while I'd been such a wimp, so stuck in my ways of hiding and repressing. But now someone needed my help.

"Good," he said. "What do you want to turn into?"

Smaller things were easier. We'd tried a house cat back at his place in Ireland. I'd gotten as far as growing furry paws before I'd passed out from the effort. It'd been weird.

"Something smallish, but fierce," I said. As the Origin, Aidan could turn into anything, so I could just mirror his Origin powers and pick whatever animal I wanted. "How about a bobcat?"

"Good choice. Do you want me to turn into one first to make it easier?"

"No. I'm just going to try to mirror your Origin power and go from there. That's more like what would happen if we were in battle. I wouldn't be able to ask you to change first."

He nodded.

I sucked in a deep breath and stepped back, then closed my eyes. Shifting was hard because it wasn't my natural state. I was Magica, so when I mirrored another Magica's powers, that came more naturally. I understood how to use magic, even if the powers were all different. But understanding how to *be* magic—to change into an animal like a Shifter did—that was harder.

I focused on the feel of Aidan's magic, which was surging now that we were actually going to use it. The sound of crashing waves and the scent of the forest filled my senses. My magic wound around his, reaching and poking, trying to get a handle on how he turned into an animal. I could feel his Elemental Mage powers. It'd be nothing to latch on to those and send a blast of fire from my fingertips.

But I bypassed it, searching until I found the wild part of his magic. It roared and surged against my own, a beast with no form. I harnessed it, envisioning the bobcat I would become, and used it to fuel the transformation.

Pain tore through me as I tried to force the change. My muscles cramped and my bones ached as they tried to reform into the shape of a cat. Sweat poured down my face.

Damn, this was hard. Aidan had said it would become easier and faster with practice—his change was nearly instantaneous—but I wasn't even close yet.

I dropped to my knees, praying I was changing. But my vision blurred, blackening at the edges.

The last thing I heard was Aidan's concerned shout.

CHAPTER SIX

A distant beeping tore me from sleep. I dragged my hand across my eyes and sat up. The room was still dark, but the unfamiliar scent made it clear I wasn't in my own bed. I woke up fully, the foreign location putting me on guard.

Oh right. I was in Aidan's childhood home. The beeping must be his alarm.

How had I gotten into bed? The last thing I remembered was trying to transform into a bobcat.

I must have failed again. Disappointment streaked through me.

No. I didn't have time to wallow in that. The sun would be rising soon. We needed to be at the Dawn Temple before that.

A knock sounded at the bedroom door. Adain's voice followed. "You up?"

"Yeah. Be out in a sec."

I hopped out of bed and pulled clothes out of the bag I'd brought, wishing desperately for a shower. There was a little bathroom out in the hall with a tiny shower, but I didn't want to take the time. I dressed and strapped my daggers to my thighs, then put Amara's thin, scruffy bunny in the inside pocket of my jacket. With a last glance around the room, I grabbed my bag and headed into the main room.

Aidan was in the kitchen, packing a couple backpacks full of food and blankets for when we reached Amara. Our kiss last night flashed through my mind. I tried to kill the blush that heated my cheeks.

"What happened last night?" I asked.

"You passed out again. Like last time."

The memory of passing out on his lawn in Ireland replaced any thoughts of last night's kiss. "Damn. I'm not getting any better."

"Not true. You were almost there when you lost it. You'll get it."

"I hope so."

Aidan swung the backpacks over his shoulders and picked up the cooler. "Ready?"

"Yeah." I grabbed the last bag off the counter and followed him out the door. The night was even colder than it had been earlier, the chill of dawn biting through my leather jacket. The moon was nearly full. The heavy cloud cover from earlier had passed. It'd give us a bit more light as we climbed up to the Dawn Temple.

We tossed the bags in the car and got in.

"So, you put me to bed," I said as he navigated down the bumpy gravel road.

"Least I could do."

"Thanks." I almost sighed in relief when we crossed the border of his family's land. I'd almost gotten used to the cloying protection spells. Getting out of there was like taking off fancy clothes—you didn't realize how uncomfortable you'd been until you were out of them.

We were silent as we drove through the mountains. We passed no other cars, just a few sheep. Their eyes glowed green if the car headlights caught them at the right angle and it was creepy as hell.

My mind was wrapped up with worry over Amara, but I could still feel the tug of my dragon sense. She was still at the Dawn Temple. I *would* get to her in time.

Tension tightened my muscles when we pulled to a stop along the road.

Aidan glanced at his watch. "Twenty minutes until dawn."

"Okay. Let's head up there and see if we can get a clue for exactly how to get in once the protections drop. The dawn sun should reveal it."

At least, that's how it'd been at the two other temples I'd raided. I couldn't help but be nervous that we wouldn't figure it out, but damn it, this was my job. I was a tomb raider. I could do this.

We climbed out of the car and each grabbed one of the backpacks. I shrugged it on and followed Aidan. We stopped in front of the stone wall that would become the entrance once the protections dropped.

"I can still feel the protection spells," Aidan said.

"Me too." They prickled against my skin like little needles, similar to the spell guarding Aidan's childhood home. "But the sun is almost up."

My foot tapped nervously as I watched the horizon. I tried to stop it, to focus my energy on the coming task, but it had a will of its own.

Finally, the sun broke over the mountain to the east. Pure light radiated, spilling over the Highlands and landing on the dome above. The prickling I'd felt from the protection spells disappeared immediately. I held my breath, my gaze darting between the dome and wall.

Finally, the wall glowed. The light coalesced into sweeping golden words. Scots Gaelic. I reached for my phone to type them in for a translation—tomb raiding was easier in the age of the internet—but Aidan spoke. "Leave this place better than you found it."

I frowned. "Better than we found it? Like, clean it up some?"

I looked around. Just pristine mountain vista. I could clean up the sheep shit, but I didn't think that was what it was talking about.

"Have you seen a riddle like this before?" Aidan asked.

"No." I chewed on my lip.

Better. Better. What was better to a temple? A place with this much magic was almost alive. It would want to stay alive. "Oh! Strength. The Dawn Temple wants to be stronger. We need to feed it some of our magic to open it. It'll use the magic to enhance the protection spells."

"Smart," Aidan said.

"Yeah, the people who built these were genius." I stepped up to the wall and placed my palms on it. "Do this. Push some of your power into the wall."

He joined me, laying his big hands next to mine. I closed my eyes and focused my magic, pushing it into the stone wall. I could feel Aidan's power surging next to me, the evergreen scent filling my nose.

My heart leapt as the stones beneath my hands began to soften, kinda like quicksand. I wanted to jerk away, but instinct made me press harder. My hands sank into the stone. My wrists followed.

"Holy hell," Aidan said.

"Just let it absorb you." My heart raced as I pushed through up to my elbows. "It'll suck us in. Our power makes us one with it and grants us entrance."

"You sure we won't get stuck?"

"Pretty sure." Still, I was a bit nervous. But no guts, no glory.

I pressed my hands harder, all the way up near my shoulders, until my hands broke through on the other side. Cool air caressed my fingertips. I shuddered to think what would happen if something was on the other side, like sticking your hand in a dark hole.

"We're good," I said. "There's space on the other side. It'll let us through. Just close your eyes and hold your breath."

"The faith I put in you." Aidan's arms sank in up to his elbows.

I stepped up to the stone, pressing my body against it. Nose to the rock. It was slightly gritty against my skin as it absorbed me. My stomach dropped in panic when I was fully enveloped, but it spat me out on the other side a moment later.

I opened my eyes.

The interior was cool and dark. I slipped on my lightstone ring and held it up to illuminate the tunnel-like hallway. The walls were made of great bricks like the entrance, but the floor was just dirt. Often, these temples were built into indentions in the mountain, half cave, half building, and they made use of the natural structure when possible.

Aidan stepped in next to me, his body pressing against my side. We could barely fit side by side in the tunnel, so we went single file. I led the way. I was the resident tomb raider, after all.

We crept through the tunnel. I kept my lightstone aloft and my ears perked.

"This place is bigger than I expected," I whispered. My dragon sense was pulling hard now, like a string around my waist. "They're ahead of us. Probably under the dome. We're nearly there."

We were so close to Amara. The faint sound of footsteps echoed in the narrow tunnel, and I stopped abruptly, shoving my hand in my pocket to dampen my light. Aidan pulled to a halt behind me.

The footsteps grew louder. Closer.

I reached for the knife at my thigh, then fisted my hand.

No. I had to use magic.

A blast of heat and smoke hit me like a freight train. I flew backward, hitting the ground hard. Fortunately— for me—Aidan broke my fall. I scrambled to my feet, drawing on my magic and reaching for Aidan's Elemental Mage powers. This area was too small for lightning.

I grasped on to flame, feeling its magic sparking hot against mine, and threw a jet of fire down the hall, head level, hoping to hit our attacker between the eyes and avoid the shorter Amara if she were there.

The jet of flame illuminated the tunnel as it flew. Right before impact, it shined upon a tall figure. No smaller bodies were nearby, thank magic. Amara must be in the dome. The flame bowled him over.

I raced toward him, Aidan on my heels.

"Good job," he said from behind.

A grin stretched across my face.

I skidded to a halt in front of the smoldering body and my smile faded. Lifeless eyes stared up out of a gray face. Narrow horns protruded from the head and stretched back along the skull.

"Shadow demon," I whispered. I hadn't thought much of the smoke. Many Magica threw smoke.

"The kind the Monster uses as henchmen, right?" Aidan said.

"Could be coincidence. There are a lot of them, and they're commonly used as mercenaries. But ignoring coincidences is a damn quick way to die."

If the Monster were in the dome, I'd feel him, right? I had to think so.

Aidan's hand gripped my shoulder. The contact brought me back from the ugly place my mind was trying to go. I dropped to my knees and checked the pockets of the demon's drab gray jacket and trousers. When my fingertips touched nothing but fabric, I scowled.

"Damn. I'd been hoping for a transport charm," I said as I stood.

Transport charms were hard to come by. Transporters like Del could make them, but it wasn't easy and took a load of power. I liked to keep them on me whenever I could—they helped you get out of a pinch real quick—but I'd used my last one a couple weeks ago. I didn't know where Shadow demons got them, but since they frequently had them, I made a point of checking their pockets.

I nudged the body with my foot. "He's dead. Let's go."

We continued down the hall. A dim light shined at the end, beckoning us.

"We're close," I whispered. My dragon sense was going nuts now, tugging me toward Amara. I wanted to sprint like hell, but stealth was our main advantage. We couldn't lose it.

I tugged off my lightstone and shoved it into my pocket. My eyes adjusted slowly to the dimness and we crept forward. Every second felt like a millennium. I didn't want to get caught in here. Far better to fight in an open space.

Aidan's hand landed on my shoulder, pressing me against the wall. I froze, unable to see but trusting Aidan's instincts.

His breath tickled my ear when he leaned down to whisper, "Main chamber ahead. I hear voices. Men and women."

I nodded and we skulked ahead. We reached the exit and peered in.

A huge circular room with a great domed ceiling spread out before us. Incredible carvings covered every inch of the walls and ceiling. If this temple had ever held any treasure, I couldn't see it. The space was empty save for the large circular ceremonial altar in the middle.

Six figures lounged on top of it, playing cards and chatting. Camp lanterns were propped up around them, spreading an inappropriately cozy glow over them. It was hard to tell, but it looked like four demons and two Magica or Shifters. From their long, white-blonde hair, the supernaturals looked to be women. Probably related.

But all the figures were adult sized. I could feel Amara here, but I couldn't see her.

"Where's Amara?" I breathed at Aidan's ear.

"To the right," Aidan whispered.

I jerked my head right and peered hard into the dark. A tiny lump huddled near the wall. It was her.

Relief filled my chest. As quietly as I could, I lowered my backpack to the ground. Aidan did the same. I reached deep for my magic, letting the crackle and pop of lightning fill me until my skin felt electrified.

I leaned to whisper to Aidan, "On three?"

"On three."

I stepped beside Aidan so we both filled the entrance. "One, two, three."

I thrust out my hands, throwing the biggest bolt of lighting I could muster right at the altar. Thunder boomed in the space, reverberating through my body. My ears rang. Aidan threw an enormous jet of flame. Heat seared me as it flew by, the golden red illuminating the domed space.

Amara shrieked. My heart ached for her, but I shoved it aside.

I raced into the room as my lightning bowled over a figure. The demon crashed to the ground. Another collapsed in a pile of flame, writhing as the flickering light devoured him.

Next to me, Aidan's form disappeared in a flash of silvery gray light. A second later, an enormous griffin stood in his place. His preferred species for shifting. No surprise, because it was scary as hell.

He roared, a noise straight from the depths of hell. Muscles rippled beneath his golden coat. His hulking form crouched low, then lunged upward, powerful wings beating the air. My hair blew back from my face. His wicked claws glinted in the low light. He swooped low and picked up a demon in his enormous beak, crunching it in half.

Three figures remained on the altar. A demon and the two blonde women. Sisters, maybe. Both dressed entirely in black with gleaming white-blonde hair flowing down their backs.

I threw another bolt of lightning, aiming for the two women. The scent of ozone burned my nose. As thunder boomed, the figures leapt out of the way, faster than a Magica.

Shifter speed.

Light swirled around the women. A second later, they transformed, their human bodies crouching low and twisting into the shapes of white wolves. Shit.

They howled, an eerie sound, then charged, heading straight for me. They were bigger than normal wolves, their coats a sleek white and their eyes glinting black. White fangs gleamed in the light from lanterns that had tumbled off the altar.

I reached deep for my magic, embracing the electric burn of the lightning. I sent a jet toward one wolf. Thunder boomed.

The streaking white bolt hit the wolf on the left. It stumbled to its knees, skidding on the stone.

Exhaustion crept up on me, but the other wolf was only a dozen feet away. I reached out for Aidan's fire gift, feeling the crackling burn of flame. The blaze erupted from my fingertips, engulfing the remaining wolf.

Behind it, Aidan dropped the last demon to the ground. Its broken body thudded and lay still.

The wolf that I'd hit with lightning staggered to its feet. Damn thing. Freaking Shifter strength. Too strong for my magic to take down in one blow. Its twin rose on shaky legs as well. Some of its fur was singed, but that was it. Both wolves swung their heads, looking from me to Aidan.

My power was running so low that I was swaying on my feet. At best, I had one more blast of flame in me. Freaking wimp.

I dug deep, pulling at Aidan's magic and wishing I could take his power as well as his gifts. I needed a battery pack at this rate.

As I corralled the flame, the wolves bolted away, racing for the altar. I blasted fire at them. The jet of orange missed the wolf by an inch, crashing into the ground. In a flash of light, one wolf transformed back into a woman. She grabbed for something on the altar, then threw herself at the other wolf. A moment later, they disappeared in a cloud of glittering silver smoke.

"Shit!"

Aidan landed next to me, his huge leonine form dwarfing mine. Blood dripped down his massive beak. Gray light swirled around him and human Aidan once again stood before me, dressed in the same clothes he'd been wearing before.

"They had a transport charm," he said.

"Yeah." The sound of Amara's weeping hit me. The bad guys were gone. We could deal with that later. Right now, I had a real problem on my hands. "Go check the entrance. See if we can still get out. I'm going to get Amara. We'll join you."

He nodded and loped off toward the exit.

I limped over to Amara. Though my bones and muscles were uninjured, my strength was dwindling rapidly. I'd used more power today than I ever had in such a short time, and boy, was I feeling it. With a shaking hand, I dug into my jacket and pulled out the plush little bunny. Its worn fur felt good against my hands. Comforting.

Amara was curled up against the wall, her dark hair hanging in her face. Her jeans were dirty and the thin sweater she wore not nearly warm enough in the cool temple. When I neared, the feel of her magic washed over me. It felt polluted...wrong. I could sense Shifter power the same way I could sense Magica power. But this was weird.

She flinched back when I neared and I winced, pushing away my concern about her magic. Maybe it was just how fear manifested for her species.

"Amara?" I lowered myself to my knees. "I'm here to help you. The Alpha Council sent me."

She shrank back. I could hardly see her face through her hair, but her breathing hitched. She was crying. My heart ached.

I held out the bunny. "Look. They gave me your rabbit. We thought you'd want it."

Her gaze darted toward the rabbit and her black eyes glimmered through the curtain of dark hair. An image of Nix when she'd been young flashed in my mind. When we'd woken in that field at fifteen, Nix had looked just like this. Stringy dark hair and wary eyes.

Anger heated my skin. Why did assholes keep using people like this? Tearing little girls away from their families and using them as pawns? I forced my fists to unclench and tried to smile. Anger wouldn't help this situation.

"I'm Cass," I said. "I really am here to help you. I wouldn't have your bunny otherwise."

She sniffled and reached out for the bunny. Quick as a snake, she snatched it to her chest. Instead of feeling better, she cried harder.

Shit. I was floundering here.

"What's wrong, honey? You're safe now. I'm going to get you out of here."

She shook her head. "The"—she hiccupped—"the Heartstone. They took it."

Right.

Shit. Double shit. That's what the woman had grabbed off the altar. Probably figured it'd be better to flee with something rather than nothing. And Amara was the keeper. Of course she'd be stressed that it was gone.

"I'm gonna get it back," I said. "I'm really good at finding things."

"Really?"

"Yeah. I found you, right? All the way in this Dawn Temple."

"Yeah, I guess you did." She sniffled her tears back.

The sound of footsteps echoed in the chamber. I turned my head to see Aidan entering. He shook his head, his expression grim, then picked up the backpacks and headed our way. I turned back to Amara.

"You hungry?" I asked. "We brought sandwiches."

Amara nodded, then shoved her hair back from her face. She scrubbed the tears from her cheeks. She looked about ten, though it was hard for me to tell ages exactly since I didn't see kids much.

"Why'd you come to get me?" she demanded.

I grinned at her tone. At least they hadn't totally squished her sass. "Because I'm good at finding things and I wanted to find you."

She gave it a second, then nodded. "All right. And you'll find the Heartstone?"

I raised three fingers. "Scout's honor. As soon as we get out of here, I'm after it."

"How's it going over here?" Aidan asked as he knelt down. "Ready for some lunch?"

Amara shot him a suspicious look. "Who're you?"

"Aidan," he said.

"What are you? I feel your power. You're strong."

"I'm the Origin."

96

Amara shrank back again, her eyes wide. "I've heard of you. You hurt the Alpha Council."

Ouch.

Aidan cursed quietly, then said, "That was my father. He wasn't a good man."

Amara frowned. "How do I know you're not like him?"

Aidan's brow creased and he scratched his chin. "Good question."

"You're really big," Amara accused.

"What if I wasn't?" A flash of gray light surrounded him. A second later, a small white mouse stood in his place. The mouse jumped up and did a flip, then an awkward mouse cartwheel.

I laughed. I'd never seen him as anything other than a griffin, and certainly not as a jumping mouse.

"Mice aren't good at cartwheels," Amara said.

"They're not. I think it's the short legs."

She nodded sagely. The mouse looked at her, then at me, and a swirl of gray light surrounded it. A second later, Aidan knelt in its place.

"I guess you're all right," Amara said. "If you're willing to be a mouse."

"Thanks," Aidan said. He reached into the bag and dragged out a blanket and a sandwich. "How about you wrap up and eat this while we find a way out of here."

Amara nodded and sat up straighter, reaching for the sandwich. Her hair swung away from her neck and a glint of sliver caught my eye.

My stomach plummeted like I was on a rollercoaster.

A thick metal collar wrapped around her neck. A big latch held it closed at the front.

Fuck. That's what the dark, sickly feel of her magic had been.

Someone had put a slave collar on her.

CHAPTER SEVEN

"How'd you get the collar, Amara?" I tried to keep my voice from shaking.

A haunted look crossed her face as she reached up to touch it. "One of the wolf women put it on me. I can't get it off. And it makes me feel kinda sick."

I bit back a curse as my stomach did flips like the mouse had. "We'll get it off."

"Now?"

"Not yet, honey." I clenched my fists. It'd kill her if we just yanked it off. "But soon, okay? Eat up while we go look for a way out of here. The main entrance is closed till tomorrow morning, but I don't want to wait that long."

"You won't leave me?"

"No way."

She nodded and pulled the sandwich out of its bag. I stood and gestured for Aidan to follow me. We walked to the altar in the middle of the temple. It was covered with scattered playing cards and snack wrappers. Like a frat party gone real wrong.

They'd been waiting here, probably to implement some kind of plan, but I didn't want to be here if they came back to finish the job.

My stomach was still lurching as I said, "We have a really big problem."

"The collar?"

I glanced back at Amara, but she wasn't paying attention. I kept my voice low. "Yeah. That's a slave collar. It's impossible for her to take it off herself. A precaution to keep slaves from killing themselves. We could take it off, but if we do, I think it'll kill her. It looks like the same kind Aaron wore."

My heart ached at the thought of the young man who'd given me his Lightning Mage powers after I'd mistakenly killed him by removing the collar. I hadn't realized what exactly it did. Could Amara's collar really be the same?

"Do you think there's any connection with the Monster who hunts you?" Aidan asked.

I shuddered. "No idea. There *were* shadow demons here. They were his chosen species of minion. And that collar looks almost identical to the one Aaron wore."

"Two similarities is two too many."

Fear felt like ants crawling over my skin.

Aidan gripped my shoulder, his touch comforting. "We'll figure it out."

"We need to do it soon. Aaron said his collar was enchanted so that his master could find him. Hers might be too."

"Shit. So right now, the wolf girl is her master. And Amara is basically wearing a tracking beacon."

"Yeah. And wolf girl is going to want her back. She's got the Heartstone, but she needs Amara to make it work."

"Now I get why she was so quick to run. She figures she can find Amara easily now."

"Yeah, true. But you were also looking at her with murder in your griffin eyes and your giant beak wide open, so I'm thinking that had something to do with her running."

He reached out and pulled me into a hug. My heart pounded as his warmth enveloped me.

"You did good with your lightning and fire. You didn't reach for your knives once."

"Thanks." I squeezed him back, then pulled away. "You're right. It's time I embraced it. I could get caught by the Order of the Magica or the Alpha Council, but right now, there are worse threats. Ones I can only beat with my powers." The image of the nearly undamaged wolves flashed into my mind. "But it takes so much magic to really damage a Shifter in animal form. I've really gotta practice my own shifting."

I needed to fight like them. Tooth and claw.

"We'll work on it," Aidan said. "In the meantime, let's see if we can blow the roof off this place. I really don't want those wolves coming back with reinforcements."

"Blow the roof off?" I cringed. To damage a place as old as this? These places were one of a kind relics from our past. They should be protected, not destroyed.

But Amara's tiny figure caught my eye. The slave collar circled her small throat. It twisted my stomach to see. The beasts who'd put it on her could come back with reinforcements. Odds were slim they'd get through the protections before dawn, but if they did, Amara would be as good as dead. A slave, possibly to the Monster who hunted me.

I'd get her out of here soon, one way or another.

"Let's get some light in this place," I said, hoping to find another way. "Aidan, you think you can conjure one of those neat fireballs? I'd try it, but I'm running on empty."

"Sure." He mimicked tossing a ball and a glowing orb of flame flew out of his hand toward the ceiling.

It hovered just below the top of the dome, casting an orange glow over the entire room. It was a bit eerie, but it was better than the dark.

Amara joined us, the blanket wrapped around her shoulders and the sandwich gripped in her hand.

"Cool," Amara said. "You're a Magica too?"

"Yeah. Got a couple skills," Aidan said.

I'll say. Like kissing. He could medal in that.

"Those carvings are cool," Amara said.

I glanced up at the decorations that covered every surface and wished I could understand them. Though they looked decorative, I'd bet my next PBR that they meant something. Recorded knowledge didn't always come in book form.

Discoloration in the stone caught my eye. *Camhanaich.* An idea tugged at my mind.

"Hey, what time is it?"

Aidan glanced at his watch. "Uh, eleven fifty."

"Good. I've got an idea. We couldn't damage the temple by blowing the stones outward, but what about modifying them. Think that's a loophole?"

I made my living through magical loopholes, what with transferring ancient spells to modern replica artifacts, so why shouldn't this work?

"Could work," Aidan said. "Especially since we gave the temple some of our power when we came in this morning."

That was a good point. All magic had a cost. It was ingenious to require temple entrants to give some of their power to make the protections stronger, but once we'd done that, we'd become a small part of the temple.

"Okay, here's my genius plan. Those colored stones spell out *Dawn*. When the dawn light hits them, the protection spell drops. What if they spelled out something different? Like Dusk, or Midday? Then, that type of sunlight would trigger the protection spells to fall. We have ten minutes until Midday."

"Nice," Aidan said.

"I thought so. Let's try it." I took stock of my power and realized I was as empty as a gas tank in a post-apocalyptic hellscape. I vowed to practice my magic more. I needed all the stamina I could get. "Actually, can you try it, Aidan?"

"Sure. But it's going to take a hell of a lot of magic. How about you two get back into the tunnel, just in case it collapses?"

"Okay, but only if you join us and do it from there." There was no way I'd let him get squashed like a bug.

He glanced at me, as if annoyed that I didn't have faith in his ability to leap out from beneath thousands of pounds of falling stone, but I just glared.

"Fine," he said.

We walked single file back to the tunnel. Amara and I got behind Aidan. I loathed standing behind a guy and letting him do the cool stuff.

"I swear to magic I'm going to practice more," I muttered.

Aidan raised his hands and directed them at the domed roof. His magic swelled.

"Your magic tastes like chocolate," Amara said.

"Shhh, hon," I said, but I grinned.

Awe filled my chest as glowing light suffused the ceiling and the stones moved. Suddenly, I realized the extent of what I'd asked Aidan to do. I'd have needed a hell of a lot more practice to manage this. Not only was he moving the stone with his elemental mage powers, he was making them hover in the air as he moved the pieces around. Did he have a bit of Telekinetic in him as well as Elemental Mage?

Finally, a new word was spelled in Scots Gaelic on the ceiling. I assumed it spelled Midday.

Aidan lowered his hands. "Okay. I'm going to grab our packs, then let's head to the gate and see if it worked. We've got three minutes until noon."

"We'll get started." I was so tired I probably needed about forty minutes to make the short walk and we only had three.

Amara reached for my hand and I took it. We set off down the narrow passage, her jostling along in the narrow space at my side. My lightstone ring illuminated our path. Fortunately, the body of the shadow demon I'd lit up had disappeared back to its hell. Aidan caught up to us a minute later.

"Right. It's noon," Aidan said when we reached the wall again.

I chewed my lip as I watched it. *Come on.* Something needed to happen.

A second later, a single stone in the middle of the wall glowed. Jackpot!

I stepped forward and pressed my hand to it. The stone grinded together, shifting outward.

"Hot damn," I said. "Thank magic it's easier to get out than in, because I've got no power left to give this place."

The sun shined brightly on the mountains as we stepped outside, and I gratefully sucked in a breath of fresh air.

Aidan dug the keys out of his pocket and tossed them to me. I barely managed to snag them out of the air.

"Get Amara to the car. I'm going to put the stones back the right way."

My heart jumped. He knew how much I hated to screw with the places I visited. "Thanks."

"Will we go home now?" Amara asked as we gingerly climbed our way down the mountain.

My stomach pitched. Damn. I'd been so focused on getting out of there and the problems with the collar that I'd forgotten about returning to Glencarrough. When I'd agreed to the job, I'd figured I could just drop her off and run. Now that she was wearing this collar, I couldn't exactly leave her. But Glencarrough was the safest place for her.

"Yeah, we're going home," I said. But I was going to need a way to get her out of this collar, and fast, because I didn't want to be hanging out at Glencarrough longer than necessary. I wanted to be hunting the monsters who'd put it on her.

Problem was, I didn't know how to take it off.

We reached the Range Rover, and I clicked the little unlock button on the keys. The car beeped and I pulled open the back door for Amara.

"Hop on in. I've got a call to make and we'll head out when Aidan gets back."

With her bunny squeezed between her arm and her body, she climbed into the car. I walked around to the front and leaned on the bumper, then reached up and pressed on the silver charm around my neck.

"Nix? Del?" I asked.

"Hey!" Nix said. "How'd it go? I've been so worried."

"She had it in the bag, Nix," Del said.

"Ah, sort of in the bag, sort of out," I said. "I've got Amara, but I've got another problem."

I told them about the collar as I watched Aidan hike back down the mountain toward me.

"So, I was thinking you could bring Dr. Garriso over here to look at it," I said. Dr. Garriso was our contact at the local museum and a scholar of all things magical history. Anything I didn't know, he usually did. "We need him right away, so I was hoping you could

106

transport him, Del, if you have enough power. Nix, you can come as a bodyguard."

"You couldn't just send a picture?" Nix asked.

"I could, but I think he's going to need to feel the magic on this thing to get a handle on it. I don't want to be right about it, but I have a feeling I am."

"Sure, we can do it," Del said. "I haven't teleported in a while, so I've got enough juice to get to you right now."

My shoulders sagged in relief. Traveling long distances took more power for Del. She regenerated what she used, but it took time. I was grateful she had enough to get to us immediately. "Thanks."

"Where should we meet you?"

"There's a little village about ten miles outside of Glencarrough. Called Kintore. Let's meet there. I don't think we should all go into Glencarrough." I thought of Amara's father who'd sensed my weird power. "Too dangerous."

"Okay, we'll be there ASAP," Del said.

"Try to make it in the next two hours if you can."

"Should be possible, if we can convince Dr. Garriso."

"Thanks. See you soon." I pressed the silver charm to turn it off just as Aidan walked up. "Let's get out of here. I need to find a battery and hook myself up because I am freaking drained."

We pulled up to the pub in Kintore about two hours later. The village was a little place, just a few houses, a pub, and a grocer, but it was cute in the way of Highland villages. It was also full of humans, so we had to lay low.

Aidan waited in the car with Amara while I went in to pick up Dr. Garriso. I didn't want her to mention Nix and Del's presence to anyone at Glencarrough. And I didn't want anyone seeing her collar.

But when I walked in, there was only one old man and his dog sitting by the fire, and both looked blind as bats. There wasn't even anyone behind the bar, but I realized why when I saw the bartender in the corner flirting with Del and Nix. Normally you'd order at the bar, but it seemed Del and Nix had inspired special treatment.

Dr. Garriso, about seventy and suited up in his tweed jacket, looked right at home in the old pub. The wooden walls, huge rafters, and gently burning fireplace looked like his natural habitat even more than his museum office. If the place was filled with books, I'd bet he'd be happy to hang out here until he turned into a ghost.

We walked over as the barman was leaving to get their drinks.

"Something I can get you, lassie?" he asked. He was tall and slender with bright orange hair, and though he wasn't my type—that seemed to be Aidan, actually—I could see why Del and Nix had flirted with him.

"Um,"—a plastic soda bottle filled with orange liquid caught my eye from the bar—"How about four Irn Brus? In bottles."

"Be right there." The barkeep smiled and walked off to the bar.

I joined the others and said, "Thank you for coming, Dr. Garriso."

His smile was warm. "Not a problem, my dear. Not often I get to jet off via tele—"

I coughed loudly, trying to cover up his slip.

Dr. Garriso's eyes widened and his bushy white brows stood up. "Oh, yes, yes. I forgot where we were. Shouldn't be talking about such things in mixed company."

Mixed company being humans. Which was why we couldn't exactly be examining Amara's collar in the middle of a pub.

I met Nix and Del's gaze. "Do you guys mind waiting here while we take Amara back to Glencarrough? Dr. Garriso can look at her, uh, necklace there."

Dr. Garriso rose to his feet.

"Sure thing." Del's gaze strayed to the barman who was carrying the drinks.

He stopped and handed me the sodas.

I winked tilted my head toward Del. "My friend here will work off the bill."

With that, Dr. Garriso and I left the pub.

I climbed into the back next to Amara, giving Dr. Garriso the front. I passed the Scottish sodas around.

"This guy is going to help us figure out how to get that collar off," I said to Amara as I handed her a bottle.

Soda forgotten, she reached up to touch the collar. Her face crumpled, tears spilling down her cheeks. The dark tar of the collar's magic washed over me, reminding me exactly what she was dealing with.

I reached over and pulled her little body into my arms, shocked at how fragile she felt. She was still just a little girl. I hadn't ever hugged one before—not since I was one myself—and she felt so damned breakable.

"I...I"—she hiccupped and gasped—"I forgot about it. With breaking out of the temple and...and you guys, I forgot. But it's still there."

"Shhh, it's okay. We'll get it off." I petted her hair, my heart feeling like it was cracking in two. Images of Aaron dying when I'd pulled his collar off flashed in my mind. I *would not* let that happen to Amara.

I held her, the sodas abandoned in our laps, until we stopped at the gates of Glencarrough ten minutes later. We both leaned toward her window, peering up at the tall wall and the many guards who gazed impassively down. On guard because they didn't have the Heartstone, I now realized.

I could almost feel Amara's joy at being back. I, however, felt like my bones were freezing from the marrow out.

Had that FireSoul been sent to the Prison for Magical Miscreants yet, or was he still locked up in their dungeon. Would the Shifters think I smelled odd this time? I shuddered, clutching Amara tighter.

The gate rumbled, rising up, and Aidan drove us slowly through. Word of Amara's return must have reached the Council, because Shifters started spilling out onto the wide stone steps of the large building in the back. They came from other buildings as well, peering anxiously at us through the car windows. Some human, some in animal form, all with expressions of relief and joy.

I pulled the blanket from the floor of the car and put it around Amara's shoulders. "Here, hon, it's cold out. Wrap up in this."

It wasn't actually cold, but she didn't question me and did as I asked. With shaking hands, I tugged the blanket around her neck until it covered the heavy collar. I didn't want everyone seeing it and whispering. That was the last thing Amara needed. They might sense that her magic was weird, but at least I could hide the collar.

Aidan parked in front of the main building and we all climbed out. Aidan and Dr. Garriso stood to my left while Amara huddled against my right. Elenora ran down the stairs, her green dress flowing behind her. She looked like a cunning medieval queen. It suited her.

"Amara!" She fell to her knees in front of Amara and hugged her.

"Aunt Elenora." Amara burrowed into her aunt's embrace.

"Your father is out searching for you," Elenora said. "But we'll call him and he'll be back soon."

Elenora's worried gaze caught my own and she mouthed, "Her eyes are black."

I pointed at Amara and whispered, "Privacy. We need privacy."

Wary understanding gleamed in Elenora's eyes and she nodded, then stood and took Amara's hand. "Come on, Amara. Let's get you some cookies."

I glanced up at Aidan, who stood beside me. He towered over the Shifters around us and concern gleamed in his dark eyes as he looked at Amara. The care he showed poked something soft in me.

I grabbed his hand, ignoring the startled look he gave me, and glanced at Dr. Garriso. "Let's follow."

The three of us set off after Elenora and Amara. Aidan squeezed my hand, his big palm dwarfing my own, as we flowed down the hall along with the rest of the Alpha Council.

We turned away from the main meeting room we'd met in the other day. Elenora handed Amara off to the rabbit Shifter I remembered from last time and they went into a room.

"Shit." I pulled away from Aidan and pushed my way through the milling members of the Alpha Council. I couldn't let Amara out of my sight. If someone took that collar off her, she'd be dead in minutes.

Fortunately, the rabbit Shifter was just helping Amara sit at a pretty little table in what looked like a children's play room.

Elenora rushed in after me. "What's wrong?"

I turned to her, trying to slow my breathing. Damn, that had freaked me out. I spoke quietly. "Amara is wearing a slave collar. If anyone takes it off, she will be dead in minutes."

Elenora paled, her green eyes going stark. "That's why her eyes are black. And her magic feels strange. Oh, fates. How?"

"Her abductors put it on her. I don't know how to get it off safely. I asked my colleague to meet us here to examine it." I nodded to Dr. Garriso, who'd come to stand by my side. "This is Dr. Garriso, scholar of all things supernatural. He works at the Museum of Magical History in Magic's Bend, Oregon."

Dr. Garriso held out his hand, his expression partially comforting, partially awkward. He didn't get out of his office much, so though he had good intentions, this was about the best he could do in any kind of difficult social situation. Elenora shook it absently, her horrified gaze darting to Amara.

"I'm going to do what I can," Dr. Garriso said. "But if you have anyone here who you think might know something about this, please, send them in. And the fewer people here when we examine it, the better."

Elenora shook her head. "No. Uh, we don't, I don't think. That's not our sort of magic."

"It shouldn't be anyone's sort of magic," Aidan growled. His hand came to rest on my shoulder, warm and comforting.

"I'm going to tell the rest of the Council to wait outside," Elenora said. "Go ahead and get started."

We approached Amara. Her eyes had gotten that haunted look again, and I wished I could turn into a mouse like Aidan. Anything to make her feel better. And it wasn't just her I was feeling for. It was my own selfish desire not to confront my past.

I shoved my dark thoughts back and said, "Amara, will you let Dr. Garriso look at that collar? He'll figure out how to get it off."

Her chin trembled but she nodded. I hadn't told her it would kill her if we just pulled it off, but apparently the Shifters who'd abducted her had made it clear.

Dr. Garriso knelt in front of Amara and inspected the collar's front clasp. My throat tightened as I watched, memories of Aaron flashing before my eyes. I'd been so stupid to take off his collar. I couldn't shake the vision of the way his skin had blackened as the poisonous magic had leeched from the collar into his body.

That couldn't happen to Amara.

Dr. Garriso was silent as he examined the collar, no doubt because he didn't want to startle her. The rabbit Shifter laid a plate of cookies in front of Amara, but the girl ignored them. Her chin quivered, as if she were trying to hold back tears.

"I'm going to look at the back now, if that is all right with you," Dr. Garriso said gently.

Amara nodded and shoved her hair out of the way. Dr. Garriso slipped around to the back of her chair and peered intently. His eyes widened, but he said nothing.

He stood. "Thank you, Amara."

"Can you take it off now?" Her voice trembled.

"Not quite yet. I'm sorry."

She started crying, the kind of panicked sobs that happened when you'd gotten yourself in a really shit situation and didn't know how to get yourself out of it.

Except Amara hadn't gotten herself into this. Some asshole had forced her into it.

"Come on, Amara. Why don't we go have a bath?" the rabbit Shifter said. Her gaze said, *So the grownups can talk.*

Dr. Garriso's sharp gaze darted to the rabbit. "It is absolutely imperative that no one try to remove that collar. And she needs guards at all times. Strong ones, preferably, who will stay close to her. Within a few feet."

The rabbit Shifter's eyes widened but she nodded. Amara's sobs grew louder, her thin shoulders shaking.

"I'm going to assign the guards," Elenora said. "Then I'll be back, and we can talk."

They led Amara out of the room as I paced, ignoring Aidan and Dr. Garriso's concerned gazes. I was like that hyper battery bunny, but I couldn't help it. There was so much energy in my body—so much desperate desire to *do something*—that I felt like I'd charged myself up with a bolt of lightning but hadn't released it.

Elenora stepped into the room. She looked at me, and her nose twitched as if she were smelling something. My stomach dropped.

But all she said was, "Please come to the council room. We'll speak there."

That just added fear to the already noxious soup of anxiety in my stomach. Just great.

We followed her out of the room.

Like before, the round table was surrounded by the Alpha Council, save for the empty seat at the head. Angus was out searching for Amara.

Fates, this whole situation sucked.

We took the empty seats, myself in the middle.

Twelve sets of expectant eyes turned toward Dr. Garriso.

"How do we get the collar off of Amara?" Elenora asked.

I immediately respected that she wanted to know how to save the girl rather than who had committed the wrong.

Dr. Garriso cleared his throat. "Well, Cass is correct. It is a slave collar. A rare variety that I've never seen before, but I'm no less certain that it is deadly. If the latch is opened to remove the collar, the poisonous magic will leak out into the body of the...ah, into Amara. It will kill her within minutes."

Rare variety? But it'd been almost identical—maybe even exactly identical—to the one that Aaron had worn.

The Monster was probably behind this. Had he arranged it so that I would be involved?

I started to tremble, unable to control the fear that streaked through me. Aidan reached over and squeezed my leg under the table. His touch calmed me enough that I stopped shaking, but the fear lingered.

"Then how can we remove it?" Elenora's voice cracked through the room.

"You can't. Not until the, ah, master is dead."

Master. Ugh. I could understand why he didn't like saying the word.

"How can you be sure it won't kill her then?" I thought of the artifacts I stole, of the ancient magic they contained that didn't disappear with the death of the one who'd placed the spells.

"This type of magic is different than your usual enchantments. It's not on the same level as a youth charm or fire spell. It is a dark, dark magic that is linked to the people involved. There needs to be a master for there to be a slave. If the master is dead, the enslaved person is free. The spell will die with the master. A bit like the free-floating magic that dies with the Magica."

Hmmm. Like Aaron's lightning cage had disappeared after I'd killed him. "But what's to keep you from killing your master if you're a slave?"

"Fear, for one. But these collars will slowly poison you if you don't do your master's bidding. It would take much longer to die, but it would be terrible. But for the most part, the master uses fear to control the slave. Sadly, it's very effective."

My stomach pitched. Poor Amara.

But it made sense now, why Aaron had said that he'd never been to his master's home. Aaron did his bidding, delivered the treasure to a drop-off point, then went out to perform another job.

Was the Monster scared of his slaves?

He'd be right to be. I'd kill the bastard who put something like that on me.

"Will this happen to Amara? If she's not with the beast who put this thing on her?" Elenora's voice was frantic.

"It could make her feel ill," Dr. Garriso said. "But unless they give her direct commands that she ignores, it shouldn't be bad enough to kill her. At least, not very quickly."

The scene of Amara and those bastards in the Dawn Temple flashed through my mind. "I don't think they've given her a command. Yet. It seemed like they were waiting. To put a plan into action or something. How long could it take to die if she disobeyed?"

Dr. Garriso's brow scrunched. "From what I have heard about other collars, it could take quite a while. It would make you sick and dampen your powers, but it takes too much power to outright kill remotely, so it would have to drain you until you died of exhaustion."

Oh, fates, this kept getting worse.

"It gets worse," Dr. Garriso said.

For fuck's sake, I couldn't get a break.

"There are runes etched into the back. They are what helped me identify the collar. But one of them is a tracking rune. The people who put the collar on Amara will be able to find her."

My heart sank. Just like I'd thought. Without the Heartstone to protect Glencarrough, they could transport right in. They might do that at any moment.

Elenora's gaze snapped to mine. "I assume you didn't recover the Heartstone, or you would have given it to me."

"Correct."

She nodded. "We would like it back, though it is possible for us to recreate it. But it would take great sacrifice on behalf of the Shifters here and quite a bit of time. Do you know who took it? Can you find them?"

"Two Shifters took Amara. Wolves. Women about twenty-five years old with white-blonde hair. It appears to be some kind of inside job."

"Two girls with white-blonde hair? About your age?" Elenora's brow scrunched.

"Do you know them?"

"Maybe. They could be Dougal's daughters." Elenora's gaze darted to Aidan.

"Shit," Aidan said.

I glanced at him.

"Dougal is one of the men my father killed. I didn't recognize the girls because they were a bit younger than me and I had no time for girls at that age, but their hair should have been a clue."

"They ran off when they were seventeen. About four years after their father's death."

"And now they want revenge," I said. So the Monster from my nightmares wasn't part of this. My shoulders relaxed. Thank fates. "But what is their plan with the Heartstone?"

"I don't know. An attack, I imagine," Elenora said. "What happened to them?"

"We killed five of their shadow demon cohorts, but they escaped with a transport charm. But I will get the Heartstone back so you can protect Glencarrough. And I *will* find a way to get the collar off of Amara."

Elenora's shoulders sagged slightly, her gaze dark.

We had to find a way around this. We'd gotten around the enchantments at the Dawn Temple. Hell, I made my living getting around enchantments. I should be able to do this.

"That's why you wanted the guards on Amara," Elenora said. "Because if those villains get ahold of a transport charm or a Transport Mage, they could waltz right in here and grab her."

"Yes."

My stomach roiled and a thin film of sweat broke out over my entire body. The thought of Amara...

No, I couldn't think of it.

"There has to be a way around this," I said. I knew the question was desperate and stupid, but I couldn't help myself. "There's no way to get it off? What if she shifts into her animal form and her neck shrinks?"

He shook his head. "The collar would shrink with her. Or expand, if necessary. The magic is very strong. It clings to that collar like lichen."

The magic…

It tugged at my mind, a gut instinct. The magic was the important part. Not the thing. The collar was just metal. It was always the magic that I hunted, never the artifact. It was why we made replicas and transferred the magic.

"What if someone else wore an identical collar? Could the magic be transferred?"

Aidan's hand gripped my leg above the knee, squeezing hard enough to almost bruise.

"Relax," I whispered.

Dr. Garriso's thoughtful gaze met mine. The rest of the council appeared to be holding their breath.

"Maybe," he said finally. "If it were identical and touching the other collar, it might be possible to transfer the spell. As long as a person was wearing the other collar and the spell could latch onto them, it might work."

So there went my hope of transferring it to an empty collar and chucking the thing in the ocean.

"Would the spell know it was on a different person?"

"Unlikely, as it isn't sentient."

"I'll try it," I said, knowing it was kind of nuts. "My sister Nix can conjure a replica and transfer the spell."

"That is above and beyond," Elenora said.

I thought of Amara, of my dream and my past.

I wanted to be the one to get those bastards. Maybe even *the* bastard. The one who hunted me. I was a freaking FireSoul, for magic's sake. I was the strongest one at this table, if I just practiced a bit. It was slightly insane that I was willing to put on the collar that would allow the Monster to track me, but that was the point. If he was coming for a slave, there was no way I'd let it be an innocent little girl. I'd rather get thrown back in his dungeon than see that happen.

Aidan's hand tightened on my knee, but I ignored him.

"I took the job. I'll finish it. I still need to find the Heartstone, so I'm going to tangle with these guys again. When I kill them, the spell will dissolve." *Then* I'd chuck the collar in the ocean. "And I've got the Origin watching my back."

"I'll wear it," Aidan said.

I glanced at him, touched and mildly peeved at the same time.

"This is my fight," I whispered. I turned to the Council and spoke more loudly. "If the bastards figure out I'm wearing it, issue commands that I ignore, and the collar makes me sick, I'll need the Origin at full strength to kill them. We're the best team for it, and this is the best way to do it."

Though I sure as hell wanted to be the person to kill them, it really was the smartest way. It was true that I *could* be the strongest one at this table because I was a FireSoul, but I wasn't. I didn't have enough practice. Aidan was the most powerful. I'd need him at full strength to protect me. Though the idea dented my pride, I'd rather be alive than stubborn.

Aidan's grip on my knee tightened but he sighed, recognizing the wisdom of my words, I'd bet.

Elenora glanced at her fellow council members. They all nodded. She drew in a deep breath. "If you're willing, then we'll accept your offer. And raise your pay. Double. You'll also have full use of any Shifter forces you need. We'll hit them hard and finish this."

I nodded. Normally, I'd be excited about the money. Right now, it was a bit hard to dredge up any enthusiasm.

CHAPTER EIGHT

Exhaustion tugged at me as I sat on the floor, my back pressed against Amara's. They'd given her a box to sit on so that our necks were at the same level. Nix had joined us twenty minutes ago, coming in from the village. She'd left Del at the pub. No need to have too many FireSouls here, even if we were helping them. We told the council Nix had traveled with a transport charm to explain her quick arrival.

Her eyes had been wide with an "oh hell no" expression as I'd told her what I wanted her to do. But eventually, she'd caved.

"Okay, Amara," Nix said. "I'm just going to use my magic to make a replica of your collar. There will be light, but you won't feel anything."

Nix's green gaze caught mine. I tried to smile, but it didn't work. I was so tired I probably looked like a ton of bricks had hit me, and to be frank, this was a dumb idea. Selfless—I'd take that credit, thanks—but dumb for anyone who wanted to live a nice, long life.

It hadn't taken Nix long to figure out why I was doing this. She'd come from the same place as me, after all. It was Nix that Amara had reminded me of when I'd first seen her, scared and huddled against the wall. Some things were more important than living a nice, long life.

Nix reached out and squeezed my shoulder, then hovered her hand near our necks. The light, floral scent of her magic surged. She'd never had my control problems, so she was more practiced with her skills. From the corner of my eye, I caught sight of the glow, but it wasn't until I felt the heavy weight of the collar squeezing my neck that I knew she was done.

My stomach pitched and rolled at the feel of it. But it would only get worse when the spell was transferred. Just the idea made me feel like a thousand-pound weight dragged at my neck.

Aidan watched from the side of the room, arms crossed over his chest and scowl fierce. I looked away. He didn't like it, but it's not like he had a choice in the matter.

"Okay, now I'm going to transfer the magic, Amara," Nix said. "It shouldn't hurt, but if it does, you need to tell me right away, okay?"

Amara's head bobbed against mine as she nodded.

As quietly as I could, I sucked in a deep breath and held it. Again, Nix hovered her hand near our necks. I strained my eyes to see, only briefly catching a glimpse of the blue smoke that usually accompanied a spell transfer.

A gross, sickly feeling spread through my body. Not really physical, but like my soul was being coated with tar. Was this what Amara had felt?

A cold sweat broke out over my skin as the feeling increased, the magic flowing into the collar. I felt polluted. Like a pond outside a sewage plant into which someone had dumped a bunch of garbage.

"Her eyes!" Elenora gasped from behind me. "They're blue again!"

That must mean mine had gone black. I swayed with exhaustion as I closed them, suddenly hating what I'd agreed to do. I wouldn't take it back, but fates, I hated it.

"Okay," Nix said. "I think it's done."

"Amara, come here," Elenora said.

The heat of Amara's back against my own disappeared. I turned to see her scurrying toward Elenora. The room seemed to spin and I grabbed Nix's shoulder, steadying myself.

"Well?" I said. "How do I look? Should I keep the eyes? Make them permanent?"

The joke felt flat on my tongue. Goofing off wasn't going to fix this, and even my delivery felt like I was half-asleep.

"Your magic feels like you jumped into a garbage can full of old cafeteria food," Nix said.

"At least I can count on you for honesty." But a small grin tugged at my lips. Nix knew I didn't like to be coddled.

"Don't worry. I'll help you take out the trash." Nix hugged me. "Honestly, I'll be fighting you for the right to tear off the bitch's head, whoever did this."

Aidan's hand landed on my shoulder. I was grateful for his warmth at my back, and also for the fact that it helped hold me upright. Amara approached, her dark eyes now blue. Her magic felt clean as well and smelled like grass.

"Thank you," she said.

"Don't thank me yet. We gotta get that ugly necklace off you." I turned to look up at Aidan, my eyelids dragging with exhaustion. Using so much magic and putting on the hell collar were more that I could handle, it seemed. "You're the strongest one here, so you've got the best senses. Do you sense any magic in her collar?"

Aidan hunkered down and reached out to touch Amara's collar. His hand looked enormous in front of her small body, but his fingers were gentle on the collar.

"It's gone," Aidan said. "I feel nothing."

Funny. Neither do I.

The next second, my vision went black as I keeled over.

The stone floor cut into my knees and the cold seeped into my bones, the ever-present chill worse now that there were only three of us left in this little cell. That meant fewer bodies to huddle with for warmth. Fewer bodies to improve the odds that I wouldn't be taken next.

They'd taken the collared girl a few days ago. A week? A month? I had no way to track time in the dark. I'd been taken on my fourteenth birthday, but I had no idea if I was still fourteen or not. I hoped so. They'd stolen so much from me. Would they steal a year of my life as well?

The girl next to me started weeping. It was hard to say what had triggered this bout, but she hadn't spoken since she'd arrived some time ago. Just wept.

Impotent rage fought with my own misery and fear. Hunger clawed at my belly as the cold gouged at my bones. What right did they have to do this to me? To lock me up like some animal? Worse, perhaps, was whatever waited for me outside this cell door.

As if I'd called upon it, the heavy wooden door swung open, crashing against the stone wall. Light blinded me and my heartbeat spiked as my stomach dropped. Sweat broke out on my skin when a massive form filled the doorway, his shoulders so broad they almost blocked out the light.

The girl next to me cried harder. The other panted. A strange growling noise rose from my throat, the sound of an animal enraged and in pain.

They would take one of us. It didn't matter if it wasn't me this time.

It would be one day soon.

The giant raised one great paw and pointed. His voice cracked like thunder. "You."

I couldn't tell who he pointed at, but it triggered something inside me. I lunged away from the wall, leaping upon him. My weight threw him to the ground with me on top of him. He wasn't as big as he looked and his magic smelled like fresh air. Too nice for the likes of a monster like him.

White noise filled my mind as I threw punches at him, hitting as hard as I could at anything I could reach. Face, neck, chest. My breath heaved through my lungs as I obeyed the beast that had taken over my mind.

Though he wasn't that big, my hits fell like rain upon him, ineffectual and weak. When one of his fists connected with my face, pain exploded. The force of his punch threw me off him. I skidded on the stone floor, blind with pain.

I scrabbled along the ground, trying to turn over, not knowing which way was up. The sound of a struggle sent strength surging through my limbs. Pain flared when I opened my eyes, but by the light of the open door, I could make out two skinny figures on top of the guard. Their fists flew as they tried to land their blows.

My friends. The only two left.

The fight was silent and eerie, as if the girls knew we couldn't be caught. This was our one chance.

A glint of silver caught my eye. A knife was slipping out of the sheath strapped to the guard's calf. Most Magica didn't carry weapons, but whatever gifts this Magica had, he found a weapon necessary.

I lunged toward him, my hand reaching for the knife. The smoothness of the leather hilt beneath my fingers was the best feeling I could remember. My fist tightened as I jerked it out of its sheath.

About eight inches long with a wicked point, it was beautiful.

The guard didn't seem to notice and he heaved a punch at one of my friends, though I couldn't tell which. Like me, she went flying, skidding along the floor. Fast as a snake, he lunged toward the other girl, throwing her to her back and leaning over her.

Rage seethed through me, a wicked fuel that gave me strength. Now.

I scrambled up the guard's legs, planting my knees on either side of his hips, and with both hands, plunged the blade into his back. It was a sickening feeling, but something in me sang with victory. He stiffened and gave a low shout.

I pulled the blade free and plunged again, rage and joy filling me as the knife sank into his flesh.

This felt good. So good. He was one of the monsters who kept us caged. Warm blood sprayed my hands as I plunged again and again, my mind a black vortex of vengeance and survival.

But as my blade flew, something else grew inside my chest. A flicker of flame, so real that it burned away the chill in my bones and replaced it with burning heat.

I was no longer a starving, freezing girl. I was the fire. A glowing white flame that consumed all in its path. And this monster was in my path. He stood between me and freedom. He had what I needed.

The flame spread from my chest through my limbs. Through rage-hazed vision, I saw the flickering white flame crawl across my skin, extending out to the man who lay dying beneath me.

Instinct compelled me, taking over my body. I dropped the blade and pressed my hands to his back. The flame was burning, raging, a magic unlike any I had ever witnessed.

But it was my magic, no matter how strange. It reached inside the man, drawn by the signature of his own power. That fresh air smell that he didn't deserve, not when he worked in this underground cage, torturing girls who'd done nothing wrong.

Ruthlessly, I plucked his magic from him, my flame burning me from within as it stole his magic and made it my own.

Power vibrated under my skin, more than I'd ever possessed. Powers that I didn't understand trilled along my nerve endings, dancing within me.

When the man was nothing but a husk beneath me, the flame that fueled me faded away. The dark and cold returned. My friends' whispers filled my ears. Dread and joy and confusion raced through me.

The door was open. We had to run, we had to—

"Hey! Wake up, Cass! Come on, you're freaking us out."

Warmth on my shoulder and a familiar voice dragged me from slumber. I thrashed, my body still on frantic auto pilot.

But when I opened my eyes, I was in a little bedroom with an adult-sized Nix and Del leaning over me, concern in their gaze. I stilled, panting. My heartbeat slowed as the sweat cooled on my skin.

I was safe. I was an adult. I was no longer in that cell.

Stealing my Mirror Mage powers.

"Holy shit." I blinked up at my friends, my brain frying with everything I'd just remembered. I struggled to sit, finding myself in the same T-shirt as before but no jeans. Just underwear.

The room was dim, with hazy sunlight shining through the thin curtains. Aidan's house. We could cover how I got here later. This was big.

"I think I just remembered how we escaped the Monster. And how I got my Mirror Mage gift."

Nix's brows shot up and Del said, "For real?"

I poked at the memories. "Yeah. At least, part of it. I definitely killed for my Mirror Mage powers, that's for sure."

I hadn't been sure up until now, though I'd always wondered if I were a real FireSoul. The kind who killed.

"Whoever it was deserved it." Del's voice was ferocious.

"Yeah, I think he did." Dread slowed my heartbeat to a rhythmic thump. "But Aaron didn't. With him, that's two people I've killed for their gifts. Maybe I'm as big a monster as everyone says FireSouls are."

Nix gripped my hand fiercely. "You're not. Aaron was dying from the slave collar anyway. He was glad when you helped him escape."

"Through death?"

Nix's shoulder lifted in a delicate shrug as her sad gaze met mine. "Sometimes that's the only way."

"Fates, that's dark."

"Life can be dark."

My mind flew back to the dungeon in which we'd spent an unknown amount of time. "Yeah. Yeah, you're right. I just hate what I've done."

"It'll take time to come to grips with," Del said. "But you've never done any of it with malice."

"Uh, I was malice personified when I killed the guard in the Monster's dungeon and took his Mirror Mage powers."

"But I bet he deserved it," Nix said.

The memory of the unknown little girl who'd worn the collar and then disappeared soon after slid into my head. I had no idea what had happened to her, but whatever it was, the people responsible deserved to be punished. In a way, I'd meted that out to the guard.

"Thanks for the faith, Nix," I sad.

"How did we escape?" Del asked.

"I'm not one hundred percent sure. We were in the same cell as my other nightmares, but this time, we attacked a guard. I stole his power, though I didn't really realize what I was doing. But right before I woke up, we were looking at the empty doorway. Like maybe we could escape."

"So we fought our way free," Del said. She grinned. "I like it."

"I don't know," I said. "I know we at least killed that guard. What happened after is still a mystery."

"Hey, maybe that's why your powers have always been so uncontrollable," Nix said. "You never had a chance to practice them. One second you got them from the guard, then the next we were on the run and somehow lost our memories."

Possible. I was improving with practice, though I wasn't close to reliable yet.

"Why the sudden surge of nightmares?" Del asked.

"No idea. Probably because I'm practicing my magic. Stirs up all the bad shit in there." I tapped my head. My hair was so stiff and gross that I almost gagged. I literally could not remember the last time I'd had a shower. It'd been run, fight, run, fight since the temple in the jungle. Was that right?

"How did I get here?" I asked.

"Well, first you passed out," Del said. Next to her, Nix mimed swooning. "Then that big hunk of man you've been trotting around with scooped you up in his giant arms."

"And carried you back to his creepy lair." Nix swept her arm around the little room.

At her words, I registered the prickle of the protection spells. I rubbed my arms.

Del glanced at the motion. "Yeah, feels like shit here. These are some grade A protections, so whoever is tracking that collar can't get within a few hundred yards of this house, but it sure ain't fun to hang out here."

"Ugh, I just want to go home," I said, glancing around the barren room. "I want a shower at my own place, a couple hours hanging out in my trove, and a PBR and a pasty at P & P's."

"No can do, buckaroo," Nix said. "Not only will that collar lead the bad guys straight to our home, but this is the safest place for you until you get that damned thing off. We gotta play it safe."

She glared at my collar. I reached up, wincing at the cold bite of the metal beneath my fingers. The cloying, sickly feel of the dark magic hadn't abated. I was glad I'd gotten it off Amara, but holy crap, it sucked.

And Nix was right. We couldn't lead them to our home. Not when I thought the Monster was involved.

"Guys?" I really didn't want to make them worry more than necessary, but this was necessary. "I think the Monster is behind this."

Their fearful gazes met mine and I explained the shadow demons and the collar. When I was done, Del and Nix both reached out and took my hands. Fear vibrated in the room.

"We'll take care of it." Nix's voice trembled.

"But he's so damned powerful," I said. Our odds of winning this—of all of us coming out alive and free— dropped exponentially if the Monster was involved. "And if the Shifter wolves can transfer the ownership of this collar, he'd be my *master*." The word made my tongue feel gross.

"We'll kill him," Del hissed. "So you won't have to worry about it."

I nodded, not convinced, but desperate to believe her.

We sat in silence for a moment, each fighting our own demons. At least I was. I figured they had to be doing the same.

"So, to try to get on a less dire subject," Nix said. "Why does your guy have such a weird place? These protections are insane, but this place is no Fort Knox. What's he protecting?"

I was grateful Nix was trying to drag us out of our fear, though not thrilled to talk about Aidan's place.

"He's got an interesting past," I said, not wanting to share more. Sure, these were my *deirfiúr*, closer than blood. But I was starting to feel loyalty to Aidan too. I didn't want to be spreading his business around.

"Hmm…" Nix said. "I don't like the sound of that. You sure about this guy?"

"Hey, you were all smoochy heart eyes about him just a week ago, throwing me at him like I was about to expire. Now you're getting cautious?"

"Temporary insanity." Nix side-eyed the room. "And it was before I came here. Normal people don't put a million dollars' worth of protective spells on their hillbilly hovels. I've literally never felt a place like this before."

I sighed. "Yeah, it's weird. But it's not his doing. It's his family's old place. Anyway, like you said, it's the safest place for me now."

I touched the collar to remind them, but all it did was send me straight into a mental diorama of all the bad shit we were now facing. Monster on my heels, slave collar around my neck, tracking spell on said slave collar.

My head spun with it all.

"We need a plan," I said. "Where's Aidan?"

"Looking for your hottie?"

"Come on, dude. Timing."

"What? I'm not freaked out by his weird little love shack," Del said. "Though I'd rather be hanging at any one of his mansions."

"Dude. Seriously? I kinda want to focus on getting this thing off me"—I pointed to my neck—"And you're cooing about Aidan?"

"Probably not the time," Nix said.

Del's blue eyes darkened and her mouth dipped down at the corners. Her voice was somber. "Yeah, I'm sorry." She sucked in a shuddery breath. "I guess I'm just not dealing with this well. The idea that you're in that thing... Of the Monster maybe coming for you. I just wish I were wearing it instead."

Warmth filled me. Del usually dealt with bad shit with jokes. And I got what she was saying. It was most of the reason I'd taken this thing off Amara. It was too hard to watch someone you loved be in such a shit situation and feel like you couldn't control it. As quickly as I'd volunteered to take this thing off Amara, I'd have been even quicker to get it off one of my *deirfiúr*.

"We'll get this off and be hanging out at P & P in no time," I said. "For now, I need a freaking shower and then we'll figure out what we do next."

"Good." Del leaned in and hugged me tight, then jerked back. "Wow, dude. You are gross."

"What? You don't like me like this?"

Nix eyed me. "I love you, but I'm going to take a rain check on my hug, cool?"

Since even I could smell myself, I had no choice but to say, "Yeah, cool."

CHAPTER NINE

After Nix and Del left the room, standing up was a hell of a lot harder than I'd expected. I was doing about a hundred times better that I had been, considering I was now vertical, but the effects of the collar were all too apparent. Felt kinda like I had the flu.

I staggered toward the door, then peered into the little hall. All clear. Since I hadn't bothered to put on jeans, the last thing I wanted to do was run into Aidan in just my underwear.

I raced into the tiny bathroom situated between the bedrooms and made quick work of my shower. It was as old and crappy as the one in my apartment, so it felt like home. When I got out, I quickly rubbed myself dry and zipped back to my little room, then changed into my last clean set of clothes.

For good measure, I strapped my daggers to my thighs. Though I was using them a lot less and no bad guys could get onto Aidan's property, they were my security blanket. I wasn't too proud to admit it. And with this collar around my neck, I'd take whatever security I could get.

I found my cell phone plugged in by the bed—thoughtful of whoever'd done that—and saw that it was late afternoon. Geez, I'd slept almost twenty-four hours.

When I made my way out into the living room, I pulled up short. Though the scene was cozy—friends and family around the kitchen table, sitting under a warm yellow light—the fact that Mathias was there was far from comforting.

I'd thought we'd left the Shifters behind at Glencarrough. Their recent obsession with my weird smell was the last thing I wanted to deal with. I was helping them out, but I couldn't be sure they wouldn't still toss me in prison for being a dreaded FireSoul.

I really couldn't get a freaking break.

"Hey! You're looking way more human!" Del said.

Aidan surged to his feet and walked toward me. He stopped, dwarfing me even more than usual. The collar's sickness made me feel puny. Normally, though I was shorter than him, I could still kick ass. But I really didn't feel like I could kick ass right now. And I freaking hated it.

Aidan cupped my face and tilted my chin so that my gaze was forced to meet his. Concern glinted in his dark eyes. The tender gesture felt weird, but nice. I wasn't used to dudes touching me like this. I could count the number of guys I'd been interested in on one hand, but I'd never given any of them the opportunity to make me feel like this before.

Like I was cherished.

I liked it.

"You okay?" His voice was rough.

"Uh, yeah." My gaze darted over his face, taking in his features with a tenderness I hadn't ever felt before. I wanted to lean in and press my lips to his. Instead, I stepped back and just said, "Thanks."

"Come on." Aidan put an arm around my waist and led me to the table. I took the seat next to his, which I noticed had been left open. Del and Nix sat across from me, Mathias and Aidan, at the head of the table, on either side.

There were yellow cans of beer and thick ham sandwiches sitting on a platter in the middle of the scarred wooden table. My stomach grumbled like an angry troll, so I grabbed one.

"Where's Dr. Garriso?" I asked right before I shoved the sandwich in my mouth.

"Sent him home on the plane," Aidan said. "He seemed to be getting antsy to return to his books. Said something about someone needing an answer."

I nodded as I chewed. Made sense. A lot of people came to Dr. Garriso for answers. There'd likely be notes shoved under his office door when he got back.

"So," I said as I eyed the beer. "I don't suppose we're going after the bad guys tonight?"

"No," Aidan said. "We need a plan. They can't get in here, so you have another night to recover while we figure out what to do."

I didn't want to tell him that I didn't think I was going to get any more recovered than this. My recovery time after using my magic had been getting shorter with more practice. A twenty-four hour nap had probably refueled me just fine.

If I looked like I needed some more recovery time, it was probably because this collar was making me feel like shit. And that wasn't going to get any better until I killed the jerk who'd put it on Amara.

"Okay, then." I tried to make my voice light. "Then I guess I'll have a beer. But I don't suppose a girl could get a can of PBR?"

Aidan grinned, then pushed one of the yellow and silver cans of beer across the table toward me. A bead of condensation rolled right down the middle of the big silver T on the side of the can.

"Try it," Aidan said. "It's better than PBR. Also refreshing and delightful."

I grinned. That's exactly how I'd described PBR to him before, though I could only remember that because it was how I described it to everyone.

"All right," I said. "Beggars can't be choosers."

And I desperately wanted to do something normal right now, like drink a beer and eat a sandwich. This would be cozy if it weren't for the fact that I wore this collar and felt like my insides were coated with tar.

I took a sip, then smiled. "Not bad."

"Refreshing and delightful?" Aidan asked.

"Refreshing and delightful," I confirmed. My grin faded as I remembered what faced us. I glanced around the table. "So, it seems I passed out and now we're all here." I glanced at Mathias. "Including you. Why are you here?"

His eyes widened. "To help, of course."

I cursed myself for my tone and the question. Obviously he was here to help. And a normal person would be grateful for the help. I, however, being very not normal, decided to verbally bite his face off.

"Thanks," I said.

"Elenora offered to let you stay at Glencarrough, but your friends refused," Mathias said. "And I can now see why, given the protections on this place. I came here to help with the planning and to coordinate any help from the Council that you might need. Manpower, assistance, that sort of thing."

"That's nice," I said, trying for normal and falling very short of the mark. *That's nice? Like I'm talking about the weather?*

He shrugged.

"So," I said. "We have an unknown number of enemies who can track and catch me if I leave the protections on Aidan's property. We also have the five of us and any assistance from the Alpha Council that we might need."

Which I didn't want to take.

"We can track them by following the Heartstone, which they have," Del said.

"It would be better if they came to us," Aidan said. "We'd have the advantage. You'd be safer."

"But we need the element of surprise. If they issue orders I can't obey, this collar will make me feel even worse." My stomach turned at the thought. I was strong enough to use my magic, but any kind of sustained physical fight would take a toll on me.

"Too bad you aren't a Shifter," Mathias said. "In animal form, the Magica spell on that collar wouldn't affect you as much."

Aidan's eyes flared with interest. I'd bet mine did as well. That was one reason to practice shifting again.

"I'm a Mirror Mage," I said. "So I could try shifting."

"Takes a strong Mirror Mage to do that, doesn't it?" Mathias said.

"Yeah. Probably not possible then. I'm fairly weak."

"I agree with Aidan," Nix said, clearly trying to change the subject away from risky territory. "We need to play it safe. Under normal circumstances, it's fine to bust in and crack skulls and see where the chips fall, but that collar changes things. Cass is more vulnerable. We'll need to limit the likelihood of her capture. Normally you could handle yourself in that situation, but not with that collar. We need to get this right the first time."

"What we need is reconnaissance," Del said. "I vote for going and checking them out."

"You would vote for that," I said wryly.

"So I like a little adventure. But really, we'll go check them out. See how much backup they have, what their base looks like."

"I could go." Mathias's yellow gaze moved to Del. "You shouldn't have to risk yourself."

Del laughed at him. "You do know I'm a demon hunter, right? I think I can handle a little recon, big man."

I grinned. Del always wanted to be the first into the fight. "I like that plan."

"Good. We'll go tonight." Nix glanced at Del. "Can you take us?"

"I can, but if we're planning for the big show to go down tomorrow, I'm hesitant to burn my power right before that. If they're far away, it'll take close to two days to refuel enough to use it again."

"Good point. Being able to bug out is handy in a fight." I looked at Mathias. "There's one super helpful thing you could do. Any chance the Alpha Council has some transport charms?"

"Of course. I'm sure I can get a couple from the armory. We have a contact with a wizard who makes them. We'll go to Glencarrough and then we can leave from there."

We? As in, he and the rest of us? Nope. I really didn't want him tagging along. I'd have to think of something to get him to stay behind on the ride to Glencarrough.

Nix, Del, and I waited in the car while Mathias and Aidan went into Glencarrough's armory. The three of us sat squished in the back, staring warily out the windows at Glencarrough's main courtyard. We'd told Mathias we had some girl things to chat about while he went into the armory, which sounded like some lame copout from a sitcom, but there was no way in hell the three of us were going to waltz through the halls of Glencarrough any more than necessary.

It was dark out, the sun having set a while ago, but there were still people walking through the courtyard. Made me antsy as a cat in a room full of rocking chairs.

"Do you think the FireSoul prisoner is still in their dungeon?" Nix whispered.

"Maybe."

"Poor bastard," Del said.

"No kidding. I can't freaking believe we're here," I said.

"Yeah, this whole deal is more serious than I thought it would be," Nix said.

Aidan and Mathias stepped out of the big wooden doors and my shoulders relaxed a bit. "Almost out of here."

They strode down the stairs, their long legs eating up the distance.

"Whew, hotties." Del fanned herself.

"Aidan is. But Mathias has made it clear he does *not* like FireSouls. There was one locked up here and he called him a filthy FireSoul."

"Ugh. Ass."

They were nearly to the car when Elenora rushed through the doors and down the stairs after them. I stiffened. She called Aidan's name and he turned, then walked to meet her at the steps. Mathias followed.

They spoke but I couldn't make out the words. Did Elenora just say FireSoul?

Nix grabbed my arm. "Oh fates, did you see that? She just said FireSoul."

Sweat rolled down my spine.

"I saw it too," Del said. "She's talking about us."

"Maybe not," I said.

"I have enough juice to get us out of here," Del said.

"Just wait." I watched Aidan nod and turned away. Mathias stayed with Elenora. "Let's see what he has to say. If it's us, get us out of here."

"Done," Del said.

Aidan strode back to the car and opened the back door. My mouth dried as I watched him.

"Elenora wants me to give my opinion on the FireSoul they have in lockup. To see if I believe his story that he's never stolen powers."

My shoulders barely relaxed. So it wasn't about us?

"Go do it," I said. "Find out what you can. We'll go do the recon and meet you back at your place."

"I'd wanted to go with you. Have your back," Aidan said.

"We got this. Go see the FireSoul. I can't hang out here any longer waiting around. It's killing me."

"All right. I'll keep Mathias with me. Elenora wants his opinion too. I'll see you back at our place." He reached out, his hand clenched around something. I held my hand under his, and he dropped two transport charms into my palms.

"Thanks. See you back at your place."

He lifted his hand like he wanted to reach out and touch me, but dropped it. "Hey, stay safe, okay?"

I smiled. "Yeah. I got these two at my back."

"Good. See you later." He turned and went back to Elenora.

"Ready for this?" I asked my *deirfiúr.*

"Like a cat's ready for tuna," Del said.

CHAPTER TEN

I clutched the transport charm as my dragon sense pulled me through the ether. Nix and Del's hands were warm on my arm. A second later, we appeared in the middle of an ancient, abandoned city. A full moon gleamed down, providing enough light to illuminate the elaborate architecture.

"Whoa," Del whispered.

"Yep." I kept my voice low and gazed at the enormous white amphitheater that gleamed in the moonlight. It was shaped like a half circle that rose up the side of a hill, hundreds of rows of seats forming an enormous staircase. "Looks Roman."

"Yeah." Nix sniffed the air. "Smells like the sea. I think we're near the Mediterranean or Aegean."

A cool night breeze blew my hair away from my face as I turned. A white stone-paved street stretched ahead of us, columns rising on either side. Behind them, fallen stone blocks and tumbled walls littered the hillside. Ruins spread out, ancient and elaborate, stretching far into the distance. Some big, some small, all made of the same white marble.

"Good place to hide out," Del said. "It's freaking huge."

"Looks like the road ends at the amphitheater," I said. "And my dragon sense is pulling me the other way, up the road. Let's follow it. And stick to the side."

There wasn't a lot of cover, but as long as we kept our ears pricked, we should be able to hear what was coming. Thank fates there was enough moonlight that I didn't need to use my lightstone ring. Del, Nix, and I edged nearer to the columns on the left side of the street and set off down the hill.

Del drew her sword. Nix flexed her hands, ready to conjure whatever weapon the circumstance called for. I focused on having my magic at the ready, hoping this wouldn't turn into a fight. The goal was recon, not battle.

"You feel that?" Del asked.

"Yeah. Strong magic," I said. The place was enchanted, but it wasn't clear what kinds of spells were lurking.

"I bet it comes alive at night," Nix said. "Keeps the tourists away, that kind of thing."

"Maybe." Unless the bad guys we were hunting had managed to enlist the enchantments to protect themselves. That would be bad.

A grinding noise sounded to my left. The hair on my arms stood up. I stilled and turned my head. Two elaborate columns rose tall along the side of the road. Part of an old gate. Each one had a figure carved on it, though the one of a warrior with an animal skin around his shoulder was in far better condition.

"Shit," Nix whispered.

The statue came to life a second later, hopping down from the pedestal. He was enormous, all massive muscle piled onto a tall frame. His white marble skin turned flesh-colored, his hair turned brown, and his clothing white and red.

"Who goes there?" he demanded in a low voice as he drew a sword from the sheath at his side.

"No one," Del said. "Who's asking?"

"Del! Let's just back away," Nix hissed. "No need to fight, they might hear us."

"Hercules," the man rumbled.

"Maybe we can work something out, Hercules." Del's tone was suggestive, and her gaze traveled up and down Hercules's very human-looking form.

"Are you seriously suggesting you'll get busy with a statue?" I whispered.

"That's freaking Hercules, dude," Del said. "And he looks human enough for me."

"Does a slattern dare enter my fair city? No one shall pass," Hercules's voice rumbled.

"Slattern?" Del's brows rose. "Oh hell no, marble boy."

Del drew her sword. The only magic I had to call on was lightning, which would be way too loud. I'd let Del handle this with her sword—silently—and step in if needed.

Nix groaned and held out her hands. The taste of vanilla indicated that she was using her magic. When things grew oddly silent, I realized she was conjuring a sound barrier around us. Good. The last thing we needed to do was alert the bad guys.

Hercules lunged, fast as a snake, swinging his blade toward Del. She parried, their steel clanging in the night.

When Del's sword lopped off Hercules's sword arm, I gave a soft shout of triumph. But Hercules didn't bleed. Instead, he bent to grab the limb, which still clutched the sword. He picked it up and held it back in place. Magic swirled and melded arm and torso back together.

Oh, hell.

He smiled and laughed low in his throat, then lunged at Del again.

"Shit!" Del said.

"This is no normal dude," I said as I drew my knives. Nix's sound barrier was good, but I wouldn't risk lightning.

Del's and Hercules's swords flashed in the moonlight. Hercules was damn good with his blade, and every blow landed with a thud. But Del was ridiculously fast, and each time his blows came close, she turned into her phantom self, her flesh disappearing until she looked like a blue apparition. But her blade couldn't connect in that form, since it too became phantom.

Hercules landed a swipe across Del's arm. She hissed. Blood dripped to the ground. I flung Righty at Hercules. It thudded into his chest right where his heart should be. He didn't even grimace.

I nicked my finger with Lefty, my blood igniting the spell that would draw Righty back to me. The dagger pulled itself from his flesh and flew toward me as I flung Lefty. I caught Righty as Lefty plunged into Hercules's chest, a centimeter from the wound that was already closing.

Again, he didn't flinch.

"Damn it!" I hissed.

Del delivered a blow that took off Hercules's arm again, but quick as lighting, he snatched it up and reattached it.

Del panted and clutched her still-bleeding arm. "This isn't working."

"Nope," Nix said. "Hang on, got an idea."

The eerie silence broke as Nix dropped her sound barrier and conjured an enormous length of chain. She tossed it to me, then flung up the sound barrier once again.

Awesome. I grabbed the heavy chain out of the air and swung it at Hercules. It wrapped around his middle twice, trapping his arms against his sides. He stumbled to the ground. An open lock was looped around one end of the chain.

Hercules bellowed.

"Lock him and gag him," Nix said as she held the barrier. "If we get away from him, the spell that made him turn to flesh might fade. He'll revert back to stone."

"Nice," I said as I ran to Hercules. I snapped the lock in place, binding him. Del tugged off her thin cotton scarf and handed it to me. I shoved it between his jaws.

He thrashed, his gaze enraged.

"Guess he's not used to losing." I stood.

"He hasn't lost yet." Nix dropped the sound barrier. "Come on."

We ran down the street. I did my damnedest to keep my footfalls silent.

"Damn." Del grabbed my arm and we stopped. "Check out Herc."

I glanced back. Hercules lay on his back, wrapped in chain with the scarf in his mouth. He'd turned back to stone. "Oh, hell. That definitely doesn't qualify as leaving things as we found them."

"We'll have to come back later, figure out how to put him back the way he was," Nix said.

"What are you gonna do?" Del asked "Convince him to stand nicely so he'll turn back into a proper statue?"

"We'll figure it out." I glanced around at the darkened street. "Come on. I don't think that's the last bad thing we're going to find."

Silently, we walked a bit farther down the street. I followed my dragon sense, which was pulling harder now that we were close. The magic that hovered over the ancient city grew, like we were reaching the center. It felt alternately malevolent or benign, but I had no idea why.

The sound of stone grinding against stone sounded again, all too familiar. My head whipped left. A statue with a head covered in snakes was shifting.

Oh shit. "Medusa!"

Nix conjured a large mirror and ducked behind it. Del and I lunged to join her.

"Fast thinking," I said. "I don't want to tangle with Medusa."

Stone grinded against stone on the other side of the mirror, then silence.

"Think it worked?" Nix asked.

"Yeah, but I don't want to look," Del said. "How about we just walk away and hope for the best?"

"Yeah."

We crept out from behind the mirror, then darted to a column, using it for cover.

"Seems clear," Nix said.

"Let's go," I said.

We crept down the street. Nothing followed that I could tell, but no way in hell was I about to look back. I'd never heard of any healer who could turn you back to human once you were stone, and I didn't want to spend the rest of my days in a museum in this tumbled down school fieldtrip.

We made our way silently along the empty street until a carving in the marble slab at my feet caught my eye.

"Hold up!" I whispered.

Del and Nix stopped, stooping over to peer at the carving.

An outline of a foot was positioned next to a woman's head and a heart.

"The woman and the heart indicate there's a brothel nearby," I said. "Not sure about the foot."

"Yeah, I think I've read about that kind of symbolism," Del said.

"This place is big. We need to be smart about this. My dragon sense is telling me they're somewhere near, but not exactly where."

"Same," Nix said. "What are you thinking?"

"This place comes alive if you trigger the magic. So the brothel might come alive."

"The main bad guys are women, though," Nix said. "And ancient Roman brothels were rarely full of dudes. At least, not dudes on that side of the transaction."

"Yeah, yeah. But these women probably have a bunch of guys working for them."

"True. Henchmen are usually dudes." Del's tone was disparaging.

"So they might be sniffing around the brothel."

Del nodded. "Yeah, that's possible. Let's check it out. That foot is the left foot. I think that means it's on the left side of the road, which agrees with my dragon sense."

We made our way a little farther along the left side of the road.

"Check it out," Del whispered, pointing left.

A marble courtyard spread out, leading away from the street. Columns rose and broken walls tumbled. But a glow came from the other side, illuminating the marble.

"Bet that's it," I said. "Come on."

We kept our footsteps silent and our backs pressed to a wall as we approached the lights. Torches. I squinted. But not real torches. They were partially transparent.

"Might I ask why you are skulking about?" a queenly voice asked.

I stiffened.

A figure appeared in front of us, a semi-transparent form draped in ancient Roman robes. Her intricately styled hair was piled high on top of her head, highlighting her beautiful features.

For a terrible second, I thought it might be a phantom, the awful apparitions that fed on fear and misery, forcing it out of their prey. Fortunately, Del was only half-phantom and didn't have a taste for misery, but that didn't make me any less afraid of the real thing.

"Are you a ghost?" Del asked.

"Indeed. Are you a Magica?"

The three of us nodded.

"Why are you trespassing upon our property?"

"Your property?" I asked.

"The brothel, of course."

Ooh, of course. She was a prostitute. A lady of the night. What was the polite term? I didn't want to offend the woman who could help us.

"We're sorry. We were just looking for something." I wracked my brain for something that wasn't exactly what we were looking for, just in case the ghost liked the bad guys.

"Not those dreadful demons or the two wolf women? Why would you fraternize with rabble like that?"

So she didn't like them. Perfect.

"Yes, actually," Nix said. "But we don't want to fraternize with them. They're threatening our sister."

I waved. "That's me."

The ghost's brows rose. "Well, that's dreadful. I presume you want to get rid of that threat? Kill them perhaps?"

Her bloodthirsty tone made me smile. "Yeah, that's pretty much what we're after. Not tonight though. Tonight is just reconnaissance."

"Perfect!" The ghost clapped her hands. "If you are trying to kill the cretins who have infiltrated our lovely abode, we can help you with that. I am Augusta. Come with me."

I glanced at Del and Nix, who both shrugged. We followed her transparent, elegant form, making our way through the torches that lined the walkway. Welcoming ghostly men to the brothel?

Augusta led us beneath a beautifully carved arch into a main entry hall. Colors and textures burst, so different than the white marble that made up everything else. Women lounged on padded benches, eating snacks and drinking wine. They were dressed in every color imaginable, chatting and reading, occasionally looking up to check us out.

I blinked, trying to take it all in, and realized that the scene was partially an apparition, like Augusta. The marble structure was real, but all the details and the people were ghostly.

"There are no men," Del said.

"Well of course there are," Augusta said. "But only the ones we want. And they're currently occupied."

Currently occupied? I caught sight of a ghostly woman leading a man into a hallway. The woman grinned at him over her shoulder.

Oh. Currently occupied *that* way.

"So you no longer run this as a brothel," I said.

"No. We're ghosts, so we have no need for coin. Now, we do whatever we like. Sometimes that includes inviting gentlemen, but not because we must." She glanced around the room. "Speaking of, Hercules is late."

Shit. Should we say something?

"Oh oh, what is that look for?" Augusta asked.

I frowned. "Um, we're sorry. We left Hercules, uh, tied up."

"Literally," Del said. "He was going to chop me up, so we restrained him."

"Would he not have chopped her up?" I asked. Had he just been waking up for his visit with the ghosts?

"Oh, he would have chopped you to little bits," Augusta said. "He's the guardian of that side. Tying him up saved your life. We'll take care of it later."

"Thank you," I said. That was a load off my mind. Figuring out how to put him back to normal without him chopping my head off would have been tough.

"Come," Augusta said. "Have a seat."

We joined her on a cushioned bench, but cold stone greeted my butt. Apparently the ghostly accessories only worked for ghosts. And possibly their statue lovers.

"So the Shifters and their henchmen are here?" I asked.

"Yes," Augusta said. "The two Shifter women have six miserable demons in their employ. They have been giving us trouble ever since they arrived."

"So they can see you."

"Yes. At night, any Supernatural who visits can see us. The demons have come sniffing around, though the women have not. We've run them off, but they're a nuisance. We want them gone."

"Where are they?" Del asked.

"The latrines, for the gods' sake."

Ew.

"There aren't many roofed structures left," Augusta said. "The latrines are essentially large benches a person could recline on, so they've been loitering there, playing cards and smoking and being generally obnoxious."

"What about the Shifter women?"

"They don't mingle with their staff. They have been seen around the old library and the houses nearby. Usually, one of the women is gone. Off hunting for something, it sounds like."

"Hunting?"

"Yes. We occasionally get a bit bored here, as you can imagine. So while we don't like the demons, we find the women to be quite entertaining. They seem clever. We have a sentry posted who lets us know what is going on. They are trying to find something. Or someone. But we don't know."

"Have they?"

"Not yet."

"The enchantments that are on this place—like Hercules and Medusa—are there many more meant to repel night visitors?" Del asked.

"Yes. Quite a lot."

"If we wanted to go spy on the Shifter women, what is the best way to get there without igniting the enchantments?" I asked.

"None, if you go alone. It's too complex to say. But I can lead you to them." Her voice was sincere, her gaze alight with excitement. No surprise. It was probably boring here after two thousand years, even if you had the run of the place and could invite Hercules over for parties."

"Thank you."

She stood. "Come on, then. Let's get started. We have a party starting in an hour, and I need to be back."

We stood and followed her, winding our way through the ruins. She led us on a circuitous path that involved edging up against a wall, threading through columns, and hopping over a tumbled stone wall. It was like a maze.

"Normally I wouldn't have to do this," Augusta said. "If the statues woke, they would leave me alone. But they wouldn't like you."

I frowned.

"Oh, I didn't intend to give offense! They wouldn't like anyone." Her voice had dropped to a whisper, and she pointed forward. "We are near the area where the Shifters linger. It was the old library. There's a small area to the right of it that is covered. That has been their base."

"Thank you," I whispered.

She led us to a broken wall that we could hide behind.

"If you peek around this wall, you'll see them just ahead, to the left a bit," she said. Her voice was so quiet it was nearly soundless. "You'll be able to get yourself out of here when you're done?"

I nodded.

"Then fair fortune. I must return to the party."

Along with Nix and Del, I waved a quick goodbye as she drifted away. The three of us glanced at each other and nodded, then crept to the vertical edge of the wall. We fell into position easily, each poking our head a tiny bit out. Del at the bottom because she was the shortest, me in the middle, and the taller Nix at the top. We'd done a lot of spying in our early days, trying to determine if places were safe enough to crash. This positioning was muscle memory by now, and we were silent as the grave.

A courtyard opened up in front of us. Directly across from our hiding spot, a set of stairs led up to a soaring stone edifice. Two stories tall, with intricate carving and many columns. The library. The rest had long since fallen away. Tumbled stones and columns littered the ground around us. To the right was a series of archways with a roof, just where Augusta had said the Shifters would be.

The two Shifter women stalked beneath it, clearly agitated. I could barely make out their voices if I strained.

"You mean you haven't told him we're late?" the Shifter on the left asked.

Him. Fear struck me like lightning.

"No! He's going to be so pissed. I'm not bringing him down on our heads any sooner than necessary," the other Shifter said. "We're not that late and he's busy. We'll get the girl, then we'll go to him. No before. Not empty-handed."

Oh, fates. Him. Him. *Him.*

Del gripped my calf and Nix grabbed my shoulder. I could feel the fear in their touch. My knees weakened slightly, the sickness from the collar and my own fear overwhelming me.

My foot nudged a small rock. It tumbled down the stairs, the sound freakishly loud in the quiet night.

"What was that?" one of the Shifters hissed.

They turned, then started walking toward us. We jerked back behind the wall. Del shoved her hand into her pocket for the Transport charm. Her eyes widened.

She couldn't find it?

Shit!

I peeked around the side of the building. A swirl of light enveloped the Shifters and they changed, charging us as wolves. Using my lightning would alert the demons that we were here. I had to keep them off us until Del found the charm or decided to transport us out of here.

I tried to keep myself hidden behind the wall so the wolf couldn't see my collar as I grabbed Righty and flung it at the wolf on the left.

Direct hit, straight into her thigh. She stumbled. I nicked my thumb with Lefty to call Righty back to me. Righty pulled itself from the wolf and flew through the air. The healthy wolf charged closer, snarling and ready to draw blood. I didn't think she could see me, but she could definitely smell the threat if she was in her wolf form.

I caught Righty and flung it again just as Del grabbed my arm.

She must have found the charm!

I called Righty back to me and caught it just as the ether dragged us away.

CHAPTER ELEVEN

We appeared in the living room at Aidan's family home a moment later. I staggered, adrenaline and the surging sickness from the collar making me feel like I'd just stepped off a Tilt-A-Whirl.

"Whew, really waited until the last minute, eh Del?" Nix asked.

Del huffed a freaked out laugh. "Yeah. I really hate to burn my transport power right before a battle. And since we weren't going to throw down there, I thought it best to find the transport charm."

"I had it under control," I said as Aidan stepped in through the front door. His hair was windswept, and his body dwarfed the small entry.

His gaze landed on me. "Glad you're back."

"Me too. Where's Mathias?"

"Sleeping in the gym. He said he likes his space."

Good, 'cause I liked keeping space between him and me. Especially after that *filthy Firesoul* comment. The memory of where Aidan had been made my stomach pitch.

"What did you find out about the FireSoul they have in the dungeon?" I asked.

"That he likely has killed for power, though I can't be sure. He was a good liar. But the Alpha Council was confident enough to consult the Order of the Magica tonight. Both governments have agreed it's best to send him to the Prison for Magical Miscreants tomorrow."

"That sucks." Del's voice was bitter.

"Damn. Okay." My heart twisted for the guy. Maybe he was actually evil, but it was disgusting he didn't get a fair trial. Just an agreement behind closed doors that it was best to imprison him for life.

"Are you feeling okay?" he asked.

"Physically, yeah." My stomach grumbled. "Beat, but manageable. Just hungry. This collar is really sapping me."

He nodded, then strode to the old fridge and grabbed one of the sandwiches left over from our dinner. He glanced over his shoulder at me. "Have a seat."

The old couch in the living room caught my eye. Way more comfortable than the table. I headed toward it, sighing as I sank down onto the plush surface. It sagged in the middle and smelled a bit dusty, but it felt like heaven to just sink in.

"I'm headed to bed," Nix said.

"Me too," Del said.

"Not hungry?" I had a feeling they were clearing the room for me and Aidan.

"Nah. Good to go." Del waved and retreated to the room I wasn't using. Nix followed.

A smile tugged at the corner of my mouth. My heart was still racing from the encounter with the wolves and what we'd learned, but I couldn't help but appreciate my *deirfiúr* who thought they were my wingwomen.

Hell, maybe they were.

Aidan walked toward me, a six pack of beer and a sandwich in his hands. "Mind if I join you?"

I shook my head. He handed me the sandwich.

As he sat, I realized that we hadn't been alone in a non-deadly environment since that kiss in his makeshift gym.

Now it was just him and me and a six pack of Scottish beer called Tennent's. Like it was a normal night. Or, magic forbid, a date night. Like the kind he'd been angling for but that I'd refused.

Why had I done that exactly?

When he grinned at me, smelling like fresh air and soap and Aidan, I had a hard time remembering the sense of self-preservation that had told me to keep my distance. Now that I was wearing this collar and staring down my mortality in a real way, I wanted to trust him. To open up to him and maybe even lean on him a little.

To be with him.

I started eating quickly. I was being stupid, mooning over Aidan when the Monster hunted me.

But that just made me want to have one normal night with him even more. Just hanging out.

Aidan waited while I finished my sandwich. Which, in fairness, was only about a minute and a half.

"Good?" he asked, a grin tugging up at the corner of his ridiculously beautiful lips.

"Yeah." I cracked open a beer and took a sip. Not bad.

Aidan reached one long, well-muscled arm behind me and gently tugged me against his side. He moved more slowly than usual, as if he were aware of his great strength in comparison to my lack. When I was well, he treated me like I could handle myself. But it seemed he followed different rules when I was sick.

As soon as his heat and strength pressed against my side, I melted into him, resting my head on his shoulder.

"That feels good," I murmured.

"Yeah, that's the truth. But how're you feeling, really?"

"Okay." The lie rolled easily off my tongue. But I didn't want to be coddled and I didn't want sympathy. Whenever I got either of those two things, I broke down. I'd found it was better to ignore the bad and just pretend everything was fine. A person could go a long way running on fumes. And I had a long way yet to go.

"I need to practice shifting," I said. "You heard what Mathias said about a Shifter's animal form. Using it to repel some of the Magica charm on this collar could do me a world of good. And I do think the Monster is behind this, for whatever reason. I need to be as strong as possible."

"Mathias is right. It's a good idea." Aidan rubbed my shoulder idly.

"And I've got to admit, the idea of sinking my claws into the bitch who put this on Amara—a little girl, for magic's sake!—is really appealing right about now."

"I'd like a piece of that myself. And you know I've always liked the idea of you learning to shift. That would give you incredible opportunities to take enemies by surprise. Or you could shift into a bird and escape."

"I like to fight my battles not run from them, thanks."

Aidan jerked and turned toward me, cupping my chin in his hand. I shivered at the intensity of his gray gaze. I hadn't seen him look so fierce outside of battle.

"I know that," he said. "You're the bravest person I've ever met. But I want you to be *safe*. For magic's sake, Cass, that's my priority above all else. And there's no shame in fleeing to fight another day."

I sighed, my heart thudding a bit harder at his words. "I know that. You're right. There are a *lot* of good reasons for me to learn to shift. I was thinking, why don't we try starting out small? Sense of smell, that kind of thing. Maybe I've been biting off more than I can chew with just trying to shift outright. It feels so different than borrowing Magica powers."

He nodded, then settled back onto the couch. "That's a good idea. But you think you can do that? Pick and choose?"

"I won't know unless I try. And those heightened senses are part of a Shifter's magic. Borrowing magic is what I do."

"Smart. But aren't you tired?"

"Yeah, but we're running out of time. We need to go after those Shifters as soon as possible. Tomorrow, even. So I have to try."

"All right. Give it a go." He glanced at the window, outside of which the sun was setting, and cocked his head to the left. "I hear a grouse in the distance. See if you can catch it."

"Can you always hear that well?" Could he hear me talking to my *deirfiúr*?

"Only when I try. Otherwise, the heightened senses are dormant. I'd go insane if I heard and smelled every little thing."

I relaxed into him, trying to ignore how good he felt so that I could focus my mind on my magic. "Okay. I'm going to try."

I was damned glad this part of my training involved sitting on my butt. This collar was weighing me down in a big way.

A sigh escaped me as I closed my eyes and reached deep for my magic. Though my instinct was to perk my ears and listen hard, that would just give me access to my own hearing, which was pretty average.

No, I had to first access Aidan's powers. My magic unfurled inside of me, a stretching and awakening that temporarily subdued the misery of the collar. My magic reached out for Aidan's power, drawn by the immense strength and ability.

His magic vibrated against my own, heightening my awareness of just how strong he was. His power hit my senses in so many different ways. Not only could I smell the predominant evergreen scent of his magic and hear the roar of waves, but I could also pick up the unique signatures of the various gifts he possessed. I was used to seeking out his Magica gifts, but this was different.

When I found the Shifter side of his power, it felt like warm fur under my fingertips. But that wasn't all. I hadn't realized until now that each of his heightened senses had its own magical signature. Perhaps this was why I hadn't had any luck shifting yet. I didn't fully comprehend the type of magic that I was trying to perform.

I'd gotten cocky.

No surprise.

I took a moment to sort through his Shifter senses until I found his gift of enhanced hearing. It sounded like a very dull thud, like my heartbeat in my ears. Maybe it was my heartbeat, I didn't know. But I followed my instinct and sank into it, eventually trying to focus on the sounds around me.

First came Aidan's breathing, deep and slow. His heartbeat, which was faster. Because I was lying against him? That's why my heartbeat was fast. Or maybe Shifters just had faster than normal heartbeats.

Eventually, I picked up the sound of the grouse, its loud, low call echoing through the night.

"I hear it," I whispered.

"Good." Aidan bent his head and pressed a kiss to my hair. "Now try smell."

I nodded and repeated the process of sorting through his magic. It was faster to find his sense of smell, but when I did, I was both delighted and disgusted. Delighted because I could smell Aidan better—soap and shampoo and the forest—but disgusted by the garbage in the trash can and the dust in the couch.

I shuddered. "Ugh."

"Yeah, the smell thing isn't always great," Aidan said. "Maybe we should have practiced that outside."

"Maybe." I let go of the enhanced sense of smell and sagged against Aidan, exhausted from that small use of power.

"Are you all right?" Aidan asked. "You seem really beat."

"Yeah. Maybe I'm still recovering from using so much at the Dawn Temple, but I don't know. I've got a bad feeling that it's an effect of the collar."

"Shit," he breathed. "But what about Aaron, the lightning mage? He wore a collar and could throw a hell of a lightning bolt."

"Good point. Maybe it takes practice to get over the feeling of having my insides coated in tar."

"You don't have a lot of time."

"One reason to practice shifting. But no more tonight. I'm beat."

"You're worse off than you said, aren't you?"

"Yeah, maybe." I didn't have the strength to hide it anymore. And I didn't want to. Not from him.

"You need to learn to trust me."

Before this week, I would have laughed. What did anyone else know about my life or why I might be a bit skeptical of others?

But after everything Aidan and I had been through, after everything he'd trusted me with…

"I'm going to try," I said.

"Then let me see if my healing can take away some of the collar's effects."

I glanced up at him, then nodded. "Okay. Thanks."

Aidan had a bit of healing gift, enough that he'd managed to mend some of my scrapes and cuts in the past. If it worked for the collar, even temporarily, I'd be all for it.

He shifted a bit so that he faced me, but kept his arm mostly around my shoulders. "Where does it feel worse?"

"Everywhere?"

"Okay. Let's start with the middle then." He laid his big palm across my stomach. The heat immediately seeped through my thin cotton T-shirt. I shivered, amazed at my ability to want him at a time like this.

His hand looked so strong and capable. Broad palm and long fingers. There were a few scars, no doubt from battles won. But it was so gentle on me.

When the healing warmth soaked into my belly, it banished the sickening darkness that the collar cast upon my soul and spread outward, reaching toward my chest and hips. I moaned, feeling as if a weight had been lifted.

"It's working?" Aidan asked.

"Mmm hmm."

Aidan slowly ran his hand up to my shoulder and then down to my hip, until most of the misery had faded away. In its place, I was left with the most overwhelming sense of Aidan. Of his powerful hands on me and his handsome face near mine.

His lips were so close that I could just lean up and taste them.

So I did, pressing my mouth to his beautiful lips. They parted in surprise, and I took advantage, slipping my tongue inside and tasting him.

Aidan groaned, a low, masculine sound that was almost a growl. His hands tightened on my hip and shoulder, pulling me close until I was pressed against his muscular chest.

Heat zinged through me, from my lips down through my entire body. I reached up and sank my fingers into his hair, holding tight so he couldn't escape.

I almost moaned my disappointment when his mouth pulled away from mine, but then his breath ghosted my neck.

"You can tell me to stop," he breathed.

"Don't stop."

His lips pressed against my neck and burned a blazing trail down to the curve where it met my shoulder. The heat of his tongue burned.

"You taste so damned good," he muttered.

His hand traced from my hip to my back, slipping under my T-shirt and tracing over the sensitive skin. I shivered, wanting him to move faster, harder. I ached for him.

"Please, Aidan," I gasped.

"Please what?" His voice was wicked and I loved it.

"More," I moaned.

"I can't tell you how much I want to give you more." His voice was a low rasp at my ear that sent a shiver through me. A hundred dirty images of the two of us flashed in front of my mind, each more intense than the last.

Rustling sounded from the bedroom.

"Damn." Aidan lifted his head from my neck and glanced to the door. "As much as I want to do many dirty things to you, I think one of your sisters is getting up. And I think you need to sleep tonight. I'd be taking advantage otherwise."

"Advantage? I want you to take advantage!" I whispered. But he was right. My sisters were one room over. "Fine. You're right. This is a small place."

A wry smile pulled at Aidan's lips. He scooped me up and stood. "Come on. I'll put you to bed."

"Where will you sleep?"

"You're sitting on it."

"You're too tall."

"I'll make do." He picked me up.

I wrapped my arms around his neck.

In the room, Aidan flipped on the light then set me on my feet near the double bed. As soon as he removed his hands from my body, the sickening feeling of the collar came back. I pressed a hand to my chest and moaned, a pathetic sound.

Aidan grasped my shoulders to steady me. "Are you all right?"

"With your hands on me, I am. And I don't mean that in a dirty way." Healing energy radiated from him. "Whatever your healing touch is doing makes me feel a lot better."

"I'm not doing it now. Not consciously, at least."

Maybe I was in such a bad way that just touching a healer sent relief spreading through me. "Whatever it is, it feels good."

"Come on, then. I'll sleep with you."

My brows rose and I grinned. "You will?"

"Not like that," he said. "Just sleep. As much as I want to, nothing more. We'll save that until you're well. But if my touch makes you feel better, I'll just hold you while you sleep."

My chest warmed at his words. And he was right. As sexy as I thought he was, and as much as I wanted to jump his bones at the nearest opportunity, now was not the time. I really did feel like hell.

"Thank you," I said. "Go put on your pj's."

"I don't have any."

I raised my brows. "Really?"

"I'll make do."

"If you must."

When he climbed into bed next to me—dressed in sweatpants and a T-shirt—my soul felt like it relaxed. Aidan wrapped his arms around me, and a sense of contentment that had nothing to do with his healing ability swept through me.

I could get used to this.

The smell of coffee tickled my nose, dragging me from a deep slumber. I scrubbed my eyes and sat up, then glanced over at the other side of the bed. Empty.

Disappointment welled.

Wait, why?

It took a second for my sleep-addled brain to remember that Aidan had spent the night with me. My disappointment was from missing him.

At least I hadn't had any nightmares. The room was cold, and I hopped out of bed and pulled on clothes. The collar's sickness still roiled my insides, but I was feeling a bit better than last night. I guessed eight hours snuggled up with a healer like the Origin really did a body good.

When I walked out into the main part of the house, I found Nix, Del, and Aidan all fixing their coffee in the kitchen. My shoulders relaxed when I saw that Del and Nix were safe. I'd worried about them last night.

"Any chance there's one more cup left?" I asked.

"Yep," Nix said. She poured the coffee into a chipped blue mug and handed it over. "Mathias brought more food, this included."

"Bless him. Where is he?"

"Went for a morning jog," Aidan said. "Wanted to check the perimeter."

"The spell should keep folks out though, right?"

"Yeah, but it doesn't hurt to check." Aidan's concerned gaze met mine. "How are you feeling?"

"Better than last night. Still not one hundred percent Freaking raring to get this collar off."

He nodded. "We will."

"Mathias's absence gives us a chance to talk about what we found last night," Nix said.

"Yeah. And make our plan." I snagged a big muffin off a plate and carried my coffee to the scarred wooden table. Though the bran muffin looked good, I longed for one of Connor's heavenly creations. An icing-covered cinnamon bun would go down real well right about now.

"So what'd you find?" Aidan asked once we'd all sat.

His brows rose as I explained Hercules, Medusa, the ghostly brothel and the helpful ghosts.

"That place sounds pretty damned cool," he said.

"Did you miss the part about a Hercules who can't die?" Del said.

"No, but I guess working with Cass has given me an affinity for history. The fact that it comes alive there is bad ass," he said. "But yeah, I agree, if we brought the fight to them and triggered too many enchantments, we'd be in a world of hurt."

"Exactly," I said. "And it gets worse anyway."

I told him all about the Shifter women, how they were searching for something—which I figured to be Amara—and that they were probably working for the Monster.

Aidan stiffened. "Could they transfer the ownership of the collar to him?"

I shuddered, a cold sweat breaking out on my skin. He'd hit right at my greatest fear.

"Yeah," Nix said. "But they said they weren't going to contact them until they caught Amara, so we have some time to get them first."

"We need to draw them into a trap," I said. "Get them before they realize Amara isn't wearing the collar or before they transfer ownership."

"But how?" Del asked. "We'd have to plant some kind of clue to draw them to us."

"Not really," Nix said. "They're—"

The air sizzled with electricity, sending a spike of energy through me. Around the table, everyone else grimaced. The hair on my arms stood on end and I shuddered. It felt gross. Like the usual crap from the steroidal protection spells, but ten times as bad.

"What was that?" Del asked.

"Protection charms being tested," Aidan said. "By someone trying to break in."

"Well then, retract my original question," I said. "Because it sounds like they're coming straight to us."

"They can't get in," Aidan said. "Not unless we drop the spell."

"Okay. Then we have time to make a plan."

An hour later, the four of us left Aidan's house. We had a plan that would be implemented tonight after the sun went down. Mathias had gone back to Glencarrough to get some things and would be gone until evening.

We'd fight the bad guys on our turf, and this time tomorrow, I'd be home free. Back at P & P, relaxing.

Though I still felt like crap, I'd be going to the battle. Not only because I was necessary to draw them to us with the tracking runes on the collar around my neck, but because there was no way in hell I wasn't getting my pound of flesh from the bitch who'd put this on Amara.

But my Magica skills were weakened by the sickness that wouldn't let up, so we were going to practice shifting one last time. As the four of us walked into the woods behind the building that held Aidan's gym, I focused on my surroundings, trying to calm myself. The glen was cool and quiet, the trees silent sentries. Dappled sunlight fell on the grass and leaves, making the place feel like a fairy glen.

When we reached a small clearing, Aidan stopped.

"This will do," he said. "Nix and Del, if you'll take up positions on either side?"

"On it," Del said as she headed back down the path a bit. Nix headed in the other direction.

We didn't think Mathias would be back anytime soon, but we'd decided to take precautions. We'd come out here so he wouldn't feel my signature in the air as I changed, and Nix and Del would stand guard in case he came back early and decided to go for one of his runs.

"Ready?" Aidan asked as he turned to face me. He'd changed into a thin blue sweater and jeans and looked like he fit right into the wilderness. In a *handsome-man-strolling* kind of way rather than a *creepy-mountain-man-hiding-out* kind of way, which I approved of.

"Yep," I said. I widened my stance and tried to relax my muscles. Being freaked out by failure and pain wasn't going to help any.

"Start with the small things, like last night. Once you've got them, try for the change."

I nodded, then closed my eyes. I pulled on my magic, sighing when it came easily. It stretched out toward Aidan, seeking his power and twining around it.

Scent came first, the fresh smell of grass and leaves and wind. A bit of Aidan's shampoo and his distinct smell. Nix and Del, as well, though they were farther off. Two dozen meters, if I had to guess.

I startled. I could determine distance from scent? Way cool.

Enhanced hearing came next. The rustle of leaves in the wind, Aidan's breathing. A crumbly, crunching noise that I realized was Del or Nix shifting on her feet, crunching leaves as they moved.

I opened my eyes and had to blink to adjust to enhanced vision.

"The tree leaves are so distinct," I murmured.

"Yeah," Aidan said.

I closed my eyes again, focusing on the image of a fox. It seemed like a fairly easy shift. There was no way I could try a griffin, but since Aidan was the Origin, I had Noah's Ark at my disposal.

I envisioned the red fur, pointed snout, alert ears. I tried to imagine myself running through the underbrush on four paws, sniffing for enticing smells, and listening for threats.

Magic warmed me from within, spreading out across my limbs and ensnaring me in the scent of warm fur. Agony followed, streaking through me. I cried out, collapsing to the ground as pain surged. My bones felt like they were breaking apart, not to form a fox, but because my magic couldn't grasp on to an animal to become. Images of wolves, bears, ravens, rabbits, ducks, falcons, and hedgehogs, flashed through my mind, chased by dozens of other animals.

I pried my eyes open, blinking through the tears. My arms stretched out in front of me.

Wrong.

They looked so wrong. My heart galloped. One arm was human, the other a fox's leg. I cried out as pain ripped through me. Darkness stole my vision.

"Cass!"

The voice tore me from the blackness. I opened my eyes. Aidan was kneeling by my side. Only seconds had passed. I looked at my limbs. They were normal again.

"What happened?" I moaned.

"You shifted halfway again and then passed out." He helped me sit up. Pain screamed through me.

Del sprinted toward me and fell to her knees. "I heard you scream. Are you okay?"

"Uh, yeah. Just having trouble." The animals that had marched through my mind flashed in front of my eyes again. I glanced at Aidan. "I think I'm having a hard time mirroring your power because you can change into so many different things. I don't know what it feels like to change, so it's hard to feel my way through that *and* select an animal. Especially if I've never been one before. Why don't you shift?"

"Okay. Let's try it again. I'll become a fox, then you mirror that."

I nodded and stumbled to my feet, leaning heavily on Aidan.

"Are you sure you can do this?" he asked.

"I *have* to do this. If I can master it, the damned collar will let up. I'll be stronger tonight."

"I can always heal you," Aidan said.

"I want to heal myself. And I need to learn this. I need to be as strong as possible, no matter how much it hurts."

"She's right," Del said.

I gave her a wan smile, appreciating that she had my back even if it meant she was pushing me toward more pain. Our lives had been full of pain. What was a little more if it was for the greater good?

"Okay, turn into a fox," I said.

Aidan let go of my arms. Gray light swirled around him. A second later, a fox stood in his place. I closed my eyes and focused on my magic. The scents and sounds of the forest now came more easily after a bit of practice. I envisioned the fox and let my magic reach out for Aidan.

Heat and power surged through me, the scent of warm fur filling my nose. My limbs vibrated with the magic surging through them, but they didn't hurt, not like last time. I opened my eyes just as I began to fall. The forest zipped before my eyes.

I flailed my arms, but my paws hit the ground.

Paws.

Oh. I hadn't been falling. I'd been shrinking. To fox size. The scent and sounds of the forest were so detailed, so strong. I looked down at my little black feet, then over at Aidan, whose black fox eyes met mine. Del gave a whoop of joy.

Beyond her, a figure stood stock still. His golden main of hair glinted in the sun.

Shit.

Mathias. He'd been able to approach because Del hadn't gone back to her spot. I'd shifted so quickly and she'd still been here, so of course she'd watched.

Mathias's yellow eyes were so wide they looked like gold coins. He'd seen everything and was shocked as shit. Why was he so shocked? I'd told him I was a Mirror Mage.

But fear glinted in his eyes as well.

Nerves made my fur stand on end.

A swirl of gray light shined to my left. Aidan appeared, standing tall on two legs, looming over me. I panicked, wishing I was human. Magic filled my limbs, hot and strong, and a second later, I was standing on two feet.

Naked as hell.

Damn, I wasn't as powerful as Aidan so my magic had incinerated my clothes. My cheeks burned, but I shoved it away.

Whatever. At least I hadn't brought my daggers and lost them in the change.

I faced Mathias. Shock and fear still twisted his features. "Hey, Mathias. Looks like I'm a strong enough Mirror Mage to shift."

He started to walk toward me, his expression morphing into something I didn't recognize.

From behind, I could hear Nix approaching, clearly having abandoned her post when she heard the shouting.

"Here." Nix draped a conjured blanket around my shoulders.

"Thanks," I said.

Mathias had the strangest look on his face as he stopped in front of me. Fear skittered across my skin like mice feet, and the air grew thick.

Quick as a flash, he reached out and grabbed my arm as he dug into his pocket and threw something to the ground.

Glittering silver smoke burst around me. The ether sucked me away. Aidan's shout was the last thing I heard.

Half a second later, I collapsed onto a cold stone floor in a dark room. It'd all happened so fast!

"What the hell?" I demanded as I climbed to my feet.

True terror hit when I saw the barren stone walls surrounding me. One miserable 40-watt bulb hung from the ceiling.

A dungeon.

The Alpha Council's dungeon.

"I knew you smelled wrong." Mathias backed away from me. "Just like the FireSoul in the Alpha Council dungeon."

Shit.

"Yeah," I said. "But I haven't killed anyone. I'm not a bad person."

The lie burned my throat on the way out, but I had to escape this dungeon. I'd sort out whether or not I was a bad person later.

"Doesn't matter. FireSouls are evil." He turned, heading toward the closed door.

He'd taken me right into a cell. I couldn't let him alert the Alpha Council! Fear lit in my veins as I charged him. I threw myself at his back, taking us both to the floor.

He was huge and so damned strong. He rolled over, throwing me off him. I had no weapons except my magic, and lightning would have Shifters down here in a heartbeat. Instinct drove me. I reached for his lion's strength with my magic. I couldn't turn into a lion, because then I couldn't talk. But maybe I could take the powers of his muscles like I took Aidan's ability to hear and smell.

Power surged through my limbs. I scrambled to him, straddling him and holding him down. Though I could process that I was naked, my own terror and the fear and disgust I saw in Mathias's eyes made it easy to ignore my nudity.

I pressed by hands into his throat, not strangling, but holding him down with the strength I'd mirrored. He struggled, but I urged my magic onward, accessing every bit of his strength.

"I'm not trying to hurt you." I panted. "I'm not trying to hurt anyone."

"Get off me, FireSoul!"

"I promise I'm good!"

"How can anyone believe a FireSoul?"

I wracked my brain. Panic fueled me. "I could kill you if I wanted. Electrocute you with my lightning, then take your power and shift and sneak out. But there's no way in hell I would because I'm not a murderer. I've got you at my mercy to prove to you that even under threat of my very life, I won't hurt you."

His eyes were stark in his face. He was so shocked that he was listening, at least. If he fought back, I'd have a hell of a time winning this since I was only as strong as he was. No, stronger.

"Look at this collar around my throat. I'm trying to save your kin!"

His gaze darted down. Something cleared in his eyes. Fear was still there, but something I'd said had hit him.

"I'm just trying to live my life," I said. "I can't help how I was born. But I'm not evil. You've got to trust me. Let me go so I can find the people who threaten Glencarrough and Amara."

More of the fear left his eyes. After an eternity of silence, he said, "Fine. Get off me."

"Do you swear you won't turn me in?" I asked.

He nodded sharply. I gave him one last hard look and scrambled off toward the blanket. I grabbed it and wrapped it around myself, my muscles still tensed to jump him.

He sat up and bent his head into his hand, thinking.

"Mathias?" I asked.

"Give me a sec."

I waited, tense as a bowstring.

Finally, he looked up.

"Damn it, Cass. This is dangerous. You know what the Council would do with you if they knew? Do with me if they knew I harbored you?"

I thought of the guy I'd seen in shackles being led through the hall at Glencarrough. "Yeah. That's why I was hesitant to take the job. But I did, because you said lives were at stake. I came to help you. Now help me."

He grimaced.

"You got me into this, Mathias. You're the one who came to me for help. Now let me help you get Amara back, and for magic's sake, don't turn me in. The loss of the Heartstone is a greater threat to Glencarrough than I am. So just let me go."

He still looked doubtful, but he nodded. Reluctantly, but committed. "You'll have to wait here while I get another transport charm. I'm all out. We're burning through these things like firewood, but I can't risk taking you out the normal way. After that other FireSoul was here, everyone has gotten more used to the scent. You're below ground now and there's no one on this level now, so you should be okay."

I shivered. No one on this level? That meant they'd taken the other FireSoul to the prison.

"I'll wait. But hurry."

He nodded.

I sat on the cold stone, huddled in my blanket and praying I was making the right decision in trusting him. I could try to escape. But he was my best bet. And I believed him. He wasn't a very good liar, and I was very good at detecting them.

The ten minutes he was gone were some of the longest of my life. I was in the Alpha Council's dungeon, one of the places I'd feared most. This was the first stop on a one-way trip to the prison for Magical Miscreants. This was what being a FireSoul was. Even the people you helped were afraid of you and willing to toss you in prison.

When he finally returned, I was vibrating with anxiety. His eyes had calmed though, and almost all of the fear in them was gone.

That calmed me a bit. If he wasn't afraid of me, he wasn't likely to turn me in.

"Ready to go?" he asked.

"Yeah."

"Uh, sorry about bringing you here."

I couldn't tell if he was really sorry, but I'd take it.

CHAPTER TWELVE

A second later, we appeared in the driveway of Aidan's family home. Nix, Del, and Aidan were yanking open the doors of his Range Rover. They whirled to face us. As a unit, they charged Mathias.

Aidan grabbed him by the throat. "I'll fucking kill you if you hurt a hair on her head."

Del had drawn her sword and was flickering blue, she was so mad. Nix had conjured a sword of her own.

I grabbed Aidan's arm. "Put him down. He brought me back. He had to know you'd try to kill him and he brought me back anyway."

"She's right," Mathias grunted. "I'm sorry I took her. She's a FireSoul. It was instinct."

Bitterness surged inside me at his words. Instinct to throw me in a dungeon for life imprisonment. That was my reality.

"But I was wrong," Mathias said. "She's helping us. Never done us wrong. I can ignore what she is."

Aidan shook him. "Ignore? You should be praising what she is. What she is is the person who was able to find Amara when no one else could. Not even your woman Mordaca could find her. But Cass did. And now she's wearing that fucking collar to save the girl."

I'd never heard Aidan swear so much. And I sure as hell had never had a man defend me so valiantly before.

"I get it," Mathias said.

"You'd better." Aidan shook him one more time and put him down. He looked at me. "You want me to kill him? He tells anyone about you, and I'll do it."

Holy shit, Aidan was like a rabid dog. Gone was the sophisticated, powerful millionaire, and in his place was a powerful beast. The ferocity in his gaze was so like his griffin side.

"Don't kill him!" I grabbed Aidan's bicep, then thought better of shaking him. I petted his arm instead, trying to calm him. "He's on our side."

"I am," Mathias said. "I knew what I was walking into when I brought her back here. I've seen how you look at her."

Like he'd kill to protect me?

Wow.

"We need her help," Mathias said. "And she's had plenty of opportunity to hurt us and hasn't. She had good reason and a perfect opportunity to kill me ten minutes ago, and she didn't. I shouldn't have panicked. I'm sorry."

I believed his apology this time. "I believe him, Aidan. Let him go."

Aidan nodded. "Keep it in mind, Mathias. There's nothing I wouldn't do to protect her."

Time felt like it slowed. I knew he cared for me. But this was really serious.

"We're fighting tonight," Aidan told Mathias. "At sundown. Be here thirty minutes before."

Mathias nodded.

Aidan's gaze met my own. My heart fluttered. "Come on, Cass. Let's go in."

He put his arm around my shoulder, supporting me. The collar's effects hit me suddenly, my adrenaline having drained away. I sagged against him and let him lead me inside.

Nix and Del stayed outside, presumably to stare down Mathias.

"I do believe him," I said. "At least until we finish this with Amara and the Heartstone."

"I do too. With the same conditions." We reached the bedroom. He turned to face me and cupped my face in his hands.

The look he gave me flashed between ferocity and tenderness, as if he was having a hard time switching back from protector mode.

I leaned up and kissed him, putting everything I had into it. My head spun.

After a moment, I realized that it was exhaustion as well as the skill of his kiss. My knees sagged.

Aidan caught me. "All right. Let's get you into bed for a rest."

"Will you hold me?"

"Better believe it."

A few hours later, the sound of voices outside woke me. I rolled over and looked up at Aidan. His eyes were open. He didn't look like he'd slept.

But he'd stuck around to hold me.

"I think Mathias has returned," I said.

A feminine voice sounded from outside.

Claire?

A masculine voice that wasn't Mathias's answered.

Connor?

"Holy crap." I leapt out of Aidan's arms and headed out of the bedroom. He followed.

When I walked out into the living room, I stopped dead in my tracks at the sight of Claire and Connor walking into the house. Claire was dressed in her fighting leathers, her short sword strapped to her back. Connor was dressed in his usual jeans and T-shirt, but he too was armed with a sword, as well as a satchel that I had a feeling contained potion bombs he'd made. Being a Hearth Witch wasn't all cookies and coffee.

Surprise was etched all over Nix's face as she offered them a soda. They hadn't caught sight of me yet, but Mathias had. He strode over. I could feel the heat of Aidan standing at my back.

"What the hell are they doing here?" I hissed.

"I'm sorry, but they insisted on coming." He kept his voice low.

"How could they insist from all the way over in Oregon?"

He winced. "I went over to chat with them."

My brows shot up.

"I didn't tell them what you are, but I wanted to ask about you. Get a feel for where you came from. I believe you're not a bad person, but I had to see what your roots were like to make sure."

Aidan basically growled from behind me.

"So you talked to my friends?"

"Yeah. Nix and Del are too close to you to be reliable."

That meant he hadn't smelled them. Which wasn't a surprise. They'd always been more skilled with their magic than me. They didn't usually smell like anything other than regular, nonthreatening magic.

"So I guess they said I was fine?" I knew they had.

"Yeah. I didn't tell them what you were, just asked questions. Said you'd been around five years, been nothing but a friend to them. But then they wanted to know how your job was doing. I said it'd turned out tough. They insisted on coming along to help out."

"And you let them?" I tried not to yell the words like I wanted to. Instead, they came out as a strangled demand.

His yellow eyes softened. "You should take help where you can get it, Cass. It was too risky for me to get any backup from the Alpha Council, not when they're so sensitive to what a FireSoul signature smells like. Especially since we'll be fighting and you'll be using your magic. And as long as you stick to your Mirror Mage powers, there's no reason for your friends to suspect anything. And even if they did, I doubt they'd turn you in."

I could almost feel Aidan relax behind me. Mathias's concern for my wellbeing had clearly helped sway Aidan.

And Mathias was right. I knew he was right. Help was a good thing. And Claire and Connor wouldn't turn me in if they knew. But I hated to risk them knowing. I liked things the way they were. It was safer. For all of us.

Particularly since knowing meant battles.

But things were changing.

"Cass!" Claire's voice carried across the room. "How're you feeling?"

My hand lifted to my collar unconsciously.

Claire's eyes flared. "We'll get that damned thing off of you."

Warmth filled my chest and my eyes smarted. I blinked back the tears and went to her. She met me halfway, wrapping me up in a hug.

"Hey, bud." Connor strolled over, a can of Irn Bru in his hand. He wrapped an arm around me and his sister. "I second Claire's vow. We'll lay down the law on those asshats who put you in that thing."

"Thanks, guys." It was good to have my friends here. Really good. I just had to see to it that they were protected.

Two hours later, I waved a temporary goodbye to everyone but Aidan, who stood by my side at the front door of his father's old home. The sun had set twenty minutes ago and Del, Nix, Claire, Connor, and Mathias were headed out to take up position at our chosen battle location on the west side of Aidan's property.

Mathias's recon had confirmed that seven demons and the two wolf Shifters were camped outside the protective spell barrier on the east side of Aidan's property. The shifters couldn't figure out how to get in, but it wasn't going to matter.

We were bringing the fight to them. But on our terms.

"I'll be right back," I told Aidan.

"Okay. We'll leave in fifteen minutes. Give them enough time to get situated in the trees."

"I know the plan, tour guide." But I grinned and punched him playfully on the shoulder, then headed back to the room I was borrowing.

We'd spent an hour hanging out in the living room, consolidating our plan—to use my tracking collar as bait to draw them to an area where our guys were hidden in the trees and then blast the crap out of them—but I'd spent the last hour resting up in fox form. As a result, I felt pretty good. Eighty percent, easy. I could kick some serious ass at eighty percent.

When I entered the bedroom, I went straight to my bag and pulled out my daggers and their thigh sheaths. Lefty and Righty felt good in my hands. As comforting as a teddy bear. I wasn't planning to use them tonight—I'd be fully embracing my magic—but I couldn't begin to imagine going into battle without them.

I strapped them on, tugged on my leather jacket, then went into the living room. Aidan stood at the door but turned to face me at the sound of my footsteps.

"Ready to go bait the trap?" I asked.

"Yeah." He approached me, putting one hand on my waist and the other behind my neck. "You feeling all right?"

"Good," I said. "Ready to blast some demons."

"You'll do great." He bent to press a kiss to my lips. I leaned into him, relishing his strength and warmth. His kiss was chaste—one of connection rather than passion—but I didn't want it to end.

When he reluctantly pulled away, my face tried to follow his like a heat-seeking missile, but he was too tall.

"Can't leave those guys hanging out in the trees too long," he said.

"Fine. Then you'd better get to shifting, because I need a chariot."

He quirked a brow. "A chariot of fire?"

I laughed. I only vaguely recognized the reference, but I was pretty sure it veered into dad-joke territory. "Sure. I'll be throwing fire, so we'll call you my chariot of fire."

He grinned, then turned and headed outside. I followed, stepping outside just as the gray light of his magic enveloped him. It pulsed over me, the scent of evergreen and the sounds of waves wrapping around my senses.

A second later, the enormous griffin stood in front of me. I repressed a shiver, surprised that he still had the ability to scare me. He was beautiful, with a gleaming golden coat and sweeping wings, but my eye was invariably drawn to his wicked claws and deadly beak.

I swallowed hard, trying to remember that this wasn't some wild griffin straight out of fairy tale nightmares.

When his black gaze met mine, the fear subsided. This was Aidan.

He bent his front knees so that I could climb on. I gripped his warm fur and scrambled onto his broad back, settling just behind his wings. His magic crashed over me, evergreen, chocolate, crashing waves.

But the overwhelming part was the sense I got of his mind. Or aura? I didn't know what the hell it was, but it was a connection, similar to the one we'd had last time I'd ridden on his back.

I was awed by a sense of his bravery. Commitment. Loyalty. Honor. Like last time, it felt like riding on the back of a superhero. Captain America, not Iron Man. The kind of super hero who did good because he was purely good.

Oh, boy. I had it baaad.

I shook the thought away and leaned toward his perked ears to say, "Let's go kick some ass."

The party wouldn't start until I arrived and my collar drew the bad guys to us.

Aidan crouched low, then launched himself into the air. The ground fell away beneath us as the wind tore at my hair and clothes. I wanted to throw out my arms like I was on a rollercoaster, but for once in my life, good sense prevailed. I hung on tight as Aidan soared over the trees.

The cool wind blew clouds over the moon, casting the night in shadow. I reached for my power, loosing my magic so that it could seek Aidan's. I mirrored his heightened Shifter vision, letting my eyes adjust. They absorbed every little bit of light that seeped through the clouds until the night became more than shadow. I could see the leaves on the trees and a rabbit coming out of its burrow.

My skin prickled as we neared the border of his lands where the protective spells ended. When we flew over the line, it only increased, as if warning people away.

I squinted into the big oaks, searching for my friends. The moon peeked out from behind the clouds, giving me just enough light to see a bit of color. A flash of steel caught my eye—Claire with her sword. Then a hint of blue—Del in her phantom form. Gold from the left—Mathias's hair. I couldn't find Nix or Connor, but I knew they were there.

I called on my dragon sense, envisioning the Heartstone. If one of the Shifters had it on her person—which she probably would, since it was too valuable to let out of her sight—I could use my treasure radar to track their progress. I closed my eyes and focused on the Heartstone, feeling the tug at my middle.

It was near.

They were coming, skirting around the protections from the north. If Nix and Del were right, eight of them. Seven of us.

But we were much stronger magically.

Aidan hovered slightly above the trees, his wings steadily beating the night air. Rustling sounded from the north, like twigs breaking under booted feet.

A flash of movement to my left. I turned my head, catching sight of eight demons streaming into the bit of woods we'd marked as our own. More than we'd expected, but not more than we could handle. Perhaps that was what the wolf Shifter had been looking for back when Del and Nix had done recon—more backup. The demons were all big and gray—shadow demons as we'd thought. Each wore an identical silver charm around their neck. I frowned.

Behind them, the two wolf Shifters ran in their human form. Their white-blonde hair glinted in the moonlight. One had a small bag strapped to her back. I could feel the tug of the Heartstone. That was my goal. And killing both those bitches so this collar could come off.

My eye caught on the identical silver charms hanging around their necks, glinting against their black shirts.

My skin prickled.

None of them looked up, so I was still hidden.

Just as the demons ran under the trees that hid my friends, a bolt of fire flew from a particularly large oak. Claire with Fire Mage powers. The orange glow lit up the night as it plowed into a demon. He screamed, dropping to the ground and rolling in the cool grass.

The battle exploded, a dozen things all happening at once. My vantage point gave me the perfect view. Del dropped from the trees and streaked toward the demons, her form glinting blue in the moonlight. She swirled her blade like a master, going corporeal long enough to land a blow that took a demon's arm.

Spears flew from the trees, piercing one demon like a pincushion. Conjured by Nix, I had no doubt. Mathias dropped from the tree, shifting to lion form as he fell. He landed on the ground with a thud, his huge paws sinking white claws into the dirt. With a roar, he charged the demons. He caught one and tore it to shreds. Connor hurled potion bombs, nailing a demon in an explosion of green smoke and acid that ate his skin.

There were still four demons and two Shifters. I called upon my magic, ignoring the sickening feeling of the collar, and mirrored Aidan's ability with flame. Warmth enveloped my arm as I shot fire from my hand.

It streaked through the trees, a huge orange bullet headed straight for one of the demons.

Direct hit.

The demon dropped, engulfed in blazing orange.

I'd been in my share of fights, but nothing was quite as badass as flying through the air on a griffin's back while shooting fire out of my fingertips.

Most of my friends were finishing their kills or moving on to new targets. Mathias was charging the wolf Shifters, who'd held back. This would be over in seconds. We could have handled three times this number of demons, no problem.

I shot another jet of flame at a demon who guarded the wolf Shifters.

The women's gazes followed the blazing trail up to where Aidan and I hovered in the air.

One of the wolf Shifters said something, but I could barely make out the sound of her voice. The other one touched the charm around her neck. Her lips moved.

Dread settled over me a second before the world went deadly silent. Every muscle in my body froze solid. My comrades on the ground didn't move an inch. Worse, Aidan froze as well, his beating wings halting in midair.

We were statues.

Aidan and I plummeted, no longer held aloft by his wings. My heart jumped into my throat as we fell. We crashed into the ground, Aidan's stiff form driving him deep into the dirt. I rolled off his back, frozen solid.

Terror raced through me as I tried to look around, but even my pupils were frozen in place. I strained to break the magic's foul hold, but every muscle in my body was dead still. The Shifters had somehow gotten ahold of a super rare freezing charm. That was what they'd been looking for, not extra help. They'd wanted to ensure the battle would go their way. Once they located me in the collar, they'd used it.

Boots appeared in front of my face. I could just barely make out the glinting white-blonde hair above me. Behind them, a demon's body twitched.

The silver charms around their necks had made them immune, of course. My heart pounded in my ears as I strained to see them. Thank magic the charm hadn't frozen my heart muscles. But then, they thought Amara would be wearing the collar and they wanted her alive.

"Just take her," one of the Shifters said. "We're out of time."

The other bent down and roughly gripped my arm, then threw a small stone to the ground. Glittering silver smoke whooshed up around us, and the ether sucked me in.

CHAPTER THIRTEEN

I collapsed to the ground a second later. Pain shot through my skull as it cracked on something hard. I went temporarily blind while hands roughly tugged my arms behind my back and wrapped thick rope around them. My ability to move had returned, but it wasn't doing me much good in this state.

As my vision slowly cleared, I lowered my eyelids and kept my body limp as I tried to get my bearings. It was night here, wherever we were, and the moon shined upon tumbled stone ruins.

I'd hit my head on stone stairs. I blinked as my gaze traveled up them. The huge, ornate library building I'd seen when I'd spied with Nix and Del. The one with the ghostly prostitutes. Maybe they would help me.

No, of course not. They couldn't make contact with living things beyond talking.

I was in this on my own.

A boot nudged my middle. I lay still, my panicked mind hamster-wheeling for escape plans.

"How the hell did she get into Amara's collar? And what are we supposed to do with her?" one of the Shifters asked from behind me.

"I don't fucking know, Caitlyn." Panic sounded in non-Caitlyn's voice.

"He's expecting us to bring him the child. We're already two days late."

"It was his fault he wasn't available before and we had to hang out in that damned Dawn Temple."

"He won't care about that!"

Him? The Monster. My heart thudded against my ribs.

"Call him, then. Maybe he'll have some use for her, and it'll buy us some time. We can't be any later."

Oh shit.

"Hey, what the hell is going on?" I demanded.

A boot kicked me again. "Shut up."

Out of the corner of my eye, I saw her—Caitlyn, I thought—walk away. She raised her wrist to her mouth and spoke directly at a silver bracelet.

A communications charm. Damn it. My heart thundered in my chest.

"Hey, I can help you get the girl," I lied. "If you'll let me out, I'll know just how to do it."

"Are you fucking kidding?" Not-Caitlyn walked around so that I could see her and glared down at me, her blue eyes sparking. The bag with the Heartstone was strapped over her back. My dragon sense pulsed, tugging me toward the bag.

"You think I'm going to believe some scum who sides with the *Origin?*" Not-Caitlyn said.

Okay, so Elenora was probably right about who these two were. Dougal's daughters.

She tapped her chin. "Actually, if he let you ride on his back, he probably cares for you. Maybe we should kill you instead of turning you over to the boss. Let him know how it feels."

Caitlyn walked back, stopping by her sister. "Chill out, Lorena. He'll be here in a few minutes. She can't be dead when he arrives, no matter how much I'd like to see the look on the Origin's face when he realizes we killed his precious..." She frowned. "Rider? Who the hell are you, anyway? Why'd he let you on his back?"

Great. I was smack in the middle of some old blood feud, tied up with my hands facing away from my enemy so the only thing I could blast was some stairs, and these bitches wanted to either kill me or turn me over to some asshole.

This was going swimmingly.

"None of your damned business," I said as I pulled on my magic, drawing deep. They thought they'd eliminated the threat by tying my hands so I couldn't shoot them with fire.

They were *so* wrong.

I reached for my magic, sending it out toward the Shifters to get a feel for their power. There was no time to doubt myself now, just time for action.

It was the first time I'd mirrored a Shifter other than Aidan, and the muddy scent of their magic overwhelmed me. I barely resisted gagging.

But it was easy to get a handle on their wolves. So much faster than mirroring one of Aidan's many forms.

His power was so complex, but theirs was simple. One form. A cinch to mirror.

Heat and magic filled my limbs. My newly sensitive ears picked up whispers—the ghosts?—and my nose caught the scent of the nearby sea. A second later, my body shrank and twisted, singing with magic as my limbs bent to form canine legs and slip out of the restraints.

My vision sharpened, taking in the shocked expression on the Shifters' faces. I'd changed so fast even I was impressed. A growl escaped my throat as I lunged at the woman nearest me. I sank my fangs into her calf, and blood gushed over my tongue. I didn't have time to process the taste as I shook her and dropped her to her back.

I lunged for her throat, but dark magic vibrated the air. My fur stood on end and an unconscious whimper rose in my throat. I recognized that magic signature. I stumbled away from the Shifter I'd downed, almost going to my knees in fear.

A man stood at the top of the steps, only ten yards from me. He wore a suit, so benign for so much evil. His power rolled out from him, a tidal wave of strength comparable only to Aidan's. The magic that radiated from him smelled like rot and decay. It felt like bee stings against my skin and tasted like death in my mouth.

I shuddered, frozen with terror.

Run!

My mind had fractured into two parts. The woman who fought like a demon and the little girl who recognized this man's power. No. This *Monster's* power.

Because that was what he was. We hadn't mislabeled him. Magic that felt like his was the darkest kind. Evil.

Demons poured out of the portal behind him. Five. Bodyguards?

I tried to stop the whimper that rose in my throat as I watched the downed Shifter scramble to her feet. The other approached the man, her shoulders slightly slumped. She was afraid of him too.

Smart Shifter.

She pulled the Heartstone from her bag and handed it to the man. It sparkled blue in the moonlight. My dragon sense tugged, but even it couldn't pull me out of this fear-induced stupor. What the hell had he done to me in the past that I froze up in fear now?

That had never happened to me. I was the Huntress. I was action, not inaction.

The Monster gripped the Heartstone, not even bothering to acknowledge her. His gaze met mine.

Ice froze in my veins.

Recognition flared in his gaze. "Well, well. What do we have here? Doesn't your magic feel familiar, little FireSoul wolf."

His voice snaked around me, spurring me to action. I sprinted away, unable to help myself. Adult Cass— brave Cass—wanted to stay and fight. But I wasn't that woman anymore. I was scared to the pads of my wolf feet, driven by memories I didn't quite remember and instinct I couldn't ignore.

I ran, frantically searching for a hiding place. There were fallen columns and tumbled walls, but nothing big enough. I sensed light a millisecond before pain slammed into me from behind.

I skidded along the ground, my tail and back lit up with heat. He'd thrown a fireball at me. The smell of my singed fur filled my nose as pain streaked through me.

Fear drove me to my feet. I was grateful for the fact that my Shifter form repelled the worst of his magic. A few more and I'd be down for the count, but I could still run now. The wall where I'd hidden with Nix and Del on our recon caught my eye. I raced toward it, desperate for cover. Another fireball shot straight by me, singing my fur but not landing.

I crouched behind the little wall, panting and quivering, then peered around the side. The Monster walked down the stone steps. His five demon guards fanned out behind him. The Shifters had turned into wolves. They stalked ahead of him, growling, their gray muzzles pulled back from sharp white teeth.

How the hell was I going to escape? Those wolves would run me down if his fireballs didn't get me first.

Fight.

I shivered.

Fight.

I tried to shove away the fear, to surface from beneath the lake of terror that drowned me. I wasn't that scared little girl anymore.

The memory of stabbing the cell guard and stealing his powers flashed in my mind.

Maybe I was that little girl. And like her, I was going to fight.

But I couldn't do it as a wolf. I reached for my magic, imagined myself as human, and let the heat fill me. My limbs stretched and fur receded, leaving me naked but too damn pissed and scared to care.

I called upon my lightning, envisioning the hot white bolt and the crack of thunder, letting the crackle and glow fill me until my skin felt electrified. I'd use Aaron's gift against the master who had enslaved him. As Aaron had wanted.

I surged to my feet and threw out my hands, sending a jet of lighting so big that my fingertips sparked. The bolt streaked through the air as thunder boomed.

Quick as a snake, the Monster raised his hand. The lightning bounced off an invisible shield, ricocheting up into the sky. From either side of me, ghostly blue figures surged forward.

Had backup arrived?

The transparent figures of the long dead ladies of the night surged toward the Monster and his pack. Their robes and elaborate hair flowed behind them. They weren't able to make contact, but they startled him enough that I was able to call upon more lightning. I threw it toward him, immediately drawing upon more.

The Monster deflected the bolt with his shield, but the second hit. He barely stumbled though.

Damn, he was strong.

I raised my hands to try again, sweat dripping down my spine, but the Monster raised his hand and released a sonic boom. A wave of power unlike anything I'd ever felt blasted me backward.

My head cracked against the stone. Stars danced behind my eyes.

The force of his boom felt like it pulverized my insides, shattering my ribs and turning my organs to soup. My breath strangled in my lungs as I tried to suck in enough air to keep going.

As my vision began to clear, I struggled to push myself up. Something hard slammed against my throat and pushed me to the ground. Fear made my eyes fly open. The Monster loomed above me, his expensive shoe pressed against my throat.

I gagged at the feeling of being beneath his shoe. Naked. Without my weapons. Too weak to throw lightning. Rage suffused my fear, and I struggled to rise. He was too strong though, and I still too weak.

"Isn't it a pleasant surprise to see you here, FireSoul."

His voice was sickeningly pleasant, his face that of a nondescript middle-aged man. But his magic washed over me like a wave of tar, even worse than the collar at my throat.

I spat at him.

He pressed his foot down. Pain surged as my throat felt like it crunched.

"Now, now, that's not very nice. Girls should be nice, shouldn't they?"

Rage lit in my chest, hotter than a thousand suns. I tried to scream at him, but no sound could escape my throat.

"I've looked for you for years," he said. "But how lucky I am to find you here. A gift."

A gift?

"Fucck ouu." The garbled words felt good.

"That's not nice." He leaned down to grab my arm. "Come on, we'll teach you a lesson about how girls are supposed to behave."

Oh hell no. I ignored the pain screaming through my body and reached deep for my magic. It electrified my skin, but before I could release a bolt of lightning, an enormous golden blur plowed into the Monster, lifting him off me and slamming him to the ground nearby.

Aidan stood over the Monster, who sprawled on his back, the Heartstone gripped in the fist nearest me. Aidan's great claws dug into the Monster's chest. Nix appeared at Aidan's side a second later, looming over the Monster like an angel of death.

The Monster's gaze met mine, fury burning in its depths. A second later, he disappeared.

The dark stain of his magic on the air followed him, but so did the tug of my dragon sense. I focused on it, trying to locate the Heartstone or the Monster, to finish the job we'd started.

But the Heartstone was gone. Like, really gone. Nowhere on earth that I could sense. Same with the Monster.

But how was that possible?

Growls sounded from my left. The wolves approached Aidan, snarling, and crouched low to pounce. Beyond them, Mathias, Del, Claire, and Connor fought the remaining demons. Fire and steel flashed through the air. Their master had taken his portal with him, so they were left for the clean-up crew.

My gaze was drawn back to Aidan. Nix lunged at one of the wolves, a long spear in her hand. But Griffin-Aidan stood stock still, his gaze on the wolf who approached him.

He wouldn't kill her.

Of course.

His father had killed her father, but he wouldn't kill her.

I didn't have that problem. I leaned up on my elbow, tried my best to ignore the pain in my side, and sent an enormous bolt of lightning at the wolf. Thunder cracked and the white light lit up the ruins surrounding us. The wolf tumbled to its side.

As it staggered up, I sent another bolt, this one smaller. My power was waning. The wolf fell again. I'd have felt guilty if I weren't wearing this collar and couldn't remember Amara's face.

The wolf climbed to its feet. Its thick Shifter hide would keep repelling my magic.

I closed my eyes and pushed the pain to the back of my mind as I reached out for the wolf's signature. I was going to have to fight on her terms. The muddy smell of her magic filled my nose, but I resisted gagging. Power and heat filled my limbs as they shifted. Reshaping my bones and organs gave me strength, as if anything that had been wounded had now healed.

I climbed to my feet and charged her, the wind in my fur. She turned to meet me, snarling and snapping, then lunged toward me. We collided in a blur of fur and fangs. Her sharp teeth caught me in the side, but I bowled her over and snapped at her underbelly.

My lips grazed only fur as she jerked away, but I followed, vengeance and rage propelling me. I leapt upon her, going for her throat. My fangs sank deep, blood gushing over my lips and tongue. I shook my head, tearing at her flesh.

She shifted, the wolf disappearing to reveal the woman beneath me. I released my jaw and followed suit, transforming back to human. Her eyes were closed and her throat torn out, but she wasn't dead yet. Close, though.

My mind flashed back to Aaron, to taking his power as he lay dying. To the cell guard who I'd killed as a teenager. Covetousness welled within me, the dragon in my soul rising. I tried to force it back. I hadn't planned to take her power. Just to kill her.

But fire filled my soul, burning me from within. The flame spread through my limbs, licking at my skin. It raced away from me, faster than I could catch it.

I pressed my hands to her shoulders. The white flame reached out to her, sinking inside her, stealing her magic. I would take her wolf Shifter into myself. Hunger surged, a force of its own that operated outside of me. Joy flared as I stole from her.

My magic examined hers, veering away from the muddy part that reeked of betrayal and evil. It sought out the pure magic, the kind that hadn't been tainted by this woman's grief and rage, and drew it back into me.

Her wolf's enhanced senses flashed through me. Her animal connection to the earth grounded me. The bright light of her magic replaced the fiery pain that filled my body.

When the last of her life's blood drained onto the white marble, the magic in my collar died. My soul buoyed, my body stopped aching.

She'd been the one to put the collar on Amara. She'd been my *master*.

She'd deserved what she got.

I dragged a shaky hand over my sweaty brow. What had happened to me? I'd stolen her power—and I'd *liked* it. That hadn't happened with Aaron. I crawled away from her, bombarded by my heightened senses. I shook my head and forced my new Shifter senses to fade so I could think.

I'd once said that I could never steal the gifts of an unwilling supernatural. That it would destroy me.

I hadn't realized I wouldn't have a choice. The FireSoul within me had risen up, taken over. And I'd liked it. Too much.

Because I'd awoken it by embracing my magic?

I had no idea. But it scared me. Taking her power didn't bother me as much as I'd expected it to. She'd been evil. She would have sold Amara to the Monster. Now I could use her Shifter power in my fight against him.

But the fact that I'd been compelled to steal it—like an addiction I couldn't fight—freaked me the hell out. And I'd actually *liked* it? I shuddered.

I tried to shove the fear to the back of my mind, climbed to my feet, and looked around. My limbs felt like jello, so sitting would be good. Somewhere away from the Shifter's body. I found a big stone block and collapsed onto it.

My friends were polishing off the demons, and the ghosts were sitting on the steps of the great building like they were watching a soccer game. Nix was backing away from the body of the other shifter. Like her sister, she'd also transformed in death.

Aidan approached me on two legs, apparently having changed back into his human form. He tugged off his jacket and crouched down, handing it to me.

"Thanks. I really gotta practice not incinerating my clothes." I didn't care so much about being naked while I was fighting. Trying to stay alive was pretty much the only thing on my mind. But the aftermath sucked. I wasn't a huge fan of standing here stark naked. The memory of strapping my daggers to my thighs this evening flashed in my mind. Aidan had given those to me. "Damn it. I incinerated my daggers."

"Don't worry. I'll get you some new ones."

I smiled. "You don't have to do that."

"I'd like to." He reached out and helped me to my feet. My legs were still wobbly from using so much power, but at least the dark taint of the collar's magic had faded.

I reached up and pressed the latch. Tensed, I waited a second. My muscles relaxed when the thing fell to the ground, harmless.

"How did you guys get here?" I asked.

"The spell faded after a while. Though it sucked until it disappeared. Then Del and Nix tracked you. Del transported the two of us. Mathias followed with a transportation charm and brought Claire and Connor along."

"Thanks."

"Duh. Of course we'd come." Nix's voice sounded from behind me.

I turned.

She wiped her bloody hands on her jeans. "You want some pants and shoes?"

"Yeah. That would be great. This is a very undignified way to enjoy my victory."

"I don't mind." Connor grinned as he approached. The short sword at his side was coated in demon blood. His bag of potion bombs was collapsed and empty.

"Shut up," I said.

He grinned.

"Thanks for coming, though," I said. "I know it's not your usual thing."

"Doesn't mean I don't like it. Every now and again, the demons need a good beat down."

"Yeah, yeah, brother dearest. You're so tough." Claire approached with a grin, her sword now sheathed over her back. Behind her, Del stood in phantom form, chatting with the ghostly ladies of the night.

Connor grabbed Claire and put her in a headlock. She squealed.

My heart lit up like the sun. This had been a hard night, but having my friends around reminded me of the good stuff.

Nix conjured a pair of jeans, socks, and boots and handed them to me. I glared at Connor. "Turn around."

He did. But Aidan didn't.

"You too."

Aidan's gaze lingered on my face before he turned. I tugged on the jeans, socks, and boots.

"All clear," I said.

They turned to face me.

"Going commando?" Connor asked.

"Seriously, shut up, you idiot," I said.

Claire punched him. I grinned, then swayed. I'd used every bit of power I possessed and then some. I was going to need a long nap soon. Aidan wrapped his arm around me and fit me against his side, providing enough support that I could stand.

Mathias approached in human form. Like Aidan and the Shifters, he was skilled enough to not incinerate his clothes. I *really* needed to practice.

"The Heartstone is gone," I said. "I couldn't get it, and I won't be able to."

"He took it?" Mathias asked.

"Yeah. Somewhere that my powers don't follow. I can't sense him or the stone."

"Who was he?" Mathias asked.

For a split second, I thought of telling him about my past and the Monster who hunted me. But secrets came too naturally to me. Secrets kept me safe. So I told him as much truth as I could. "The Shifters didn't say. Just that they were getting the Heartstone for him. And that they hate Aidan. Elenora was right. They were Dougal's daughters. Perhaps he knew of their rage and enlisted them in some plan. Whatever it is, he wants the Heartstone for it."

Mathias nodded and stepped closer. He glanced over his shoulder at Claire and Connor, who'd walked away to join Del and the ghosts.

"I thought they looked familiar," he said quietly. "I'll pass on what you've said to the Council. It's best that you not return to Glencarrough. You're lucky you escaped without anyone connecting your scent to that of the captured FireSoul. I won't tell anyone what you are, but keep your secret close."

"Thank you." I believed him.

"And we'll see to it that you're paid in full."

"I didn't succeed."

"I'd say you went above and beyond." He eyed the collar on the ground at my feet. "And you saved Amara, the most important part of this. We'll be able to create another Heartstone, though it will take great sacrifice. It may take time, but Glencarrough will be safe again eventually."

I nodded my thanks just before my knees collapsed. Aidan swept me up in his arms. Exhaustion tugged at me.

"I don't suppose anyone has a transportation charm?" I asked. After such a long journey, Del would likely be tapped out for a while.

"I used the last," Mathias said.

Damn. It was going to be a long way home.

CHAPTER FOURTEEN

Hot water pounded down on me as I stood in the tiny shower in my apartment, washing away the grime of traveling over six thousand miles by plane, train, and automobile. We'd left the ruins in Turkey over thirty-six hours ago, but because we'd run out of transportation charms and we weren't in Aidan's sphere of influence, as I liked to call it, we'd had to rely on public transportation to get home.

No private jets or zipping across the ether.

How quickly I'd forgotten what normal travel was like. A month ago, it was all I'd used. Crammed into commercial flights and rural buses, trying to get to ancient sites. Only occasionally was I lucky enough to use a transportation charm, and really, since I only used those in emergencies, I wouldn't call them lucky.

But at least I was home. I scrubbed the water out of my eyes and grabbed the can of PBR I'd set on the little shampoo shelf. I took a swig, the cold, refreshing bubbles washing down my throat.

Ah, shower beer. The best beer, second only to beer that accompanied donuts for dinner.

I rinsed the last of the shampoo from my hair and climbed out. My tiny bathroom was cramped and ancient, but it was home and I was damned glad to be there. My beer kept me company as I walked to my cluttered bedroom and grabbed jeans and a T-shirt off the chair in the corner.

I sniffed them. Clean? Maybe. Maybe not. But they were cleaner than I'd been before my shower, so I considered them good. I'd slept most of the way home, curled up in hard little seats, but I'd be hitting the hay early tonight anyway so the clothes would only have to last me a few hours.

A knock sounded at the door. Del and Nix. After arriving in Magic's Bend, we'd all split back to our own places to clean up and lick our wounds. Because I'd been comatose most of the ride home, we'd agreed to meet up after our showers to talk about what I'd learned from the Monster.

I pulled open the door to find Nix and Del on the other side, each with a beer in hand.

"Hey," Nix said.

Del was taking a sip of her beer, so she just did that chin lift thing guys do.

"Come on in." I stepped back.

They entered and headed toward the couch in my postage-stamp sized living room.

"Nope," I said. "Let's go to my trove. I just want to relax."

They veered toward the bedroom and I followed, going straight for the section of blank wall that contained the hidden door. The enchantment unlocked at my touch and I pushed.

The door swung open and I slipped inside, flicking on the light. Calm flowed over me as the light gleamed on the rows and racks of my treasure. Leather jackets, boots, and weapons. It was weird treasure, but it was mine. Each of us had a different idea of what constituted treasure, but our dragon souls demanded that we feed the beast, hoarding it all in our troves. This was my favorite place in the world, even though I knew it belonged on an episode of *Supernatural Hoarders*.

"Looks like we'll be able to keep up the rent," Nix said as she entered.

"Thank magic," I said. We'd have a hard time finding a better place. Each of us had a floor of the old factory, about four thousand square feet each. Our living space took maybe a tenth of that. The rest was our trove, locked behind magic and illusion.

We settled on the floor near the door, leaning against the wall.

"You need a couch in here," Del said.

"Eh." I'd considered it, seeing as this was the place I always came when I needed to recharge, but hadn't done it yet. "It's just kinda weird, you know? Hanging out with our treasure, crouched on it like damned dragons."

"We are damned dragons," Del said.

"No, we're not. We just have a bit of their soul." I swigged my beer as I gazed at the weapons and leather jackets displayed on the wall across from me. "Whatever that means."

Nix and Del both shrugged. We'd speculated about it in the past, but had never figured out what it meant exactly. Was it literal? Figurative?

"But that's why the Monster is hunting us, right?" Nix asked.

"Yeah," I shuddered. I debated telling them about my compulsion to steal the Shifter's power, but didn't. I still needed to process it. What if I was as much a monster as the one who hunted us?

I thrust the thought away.

"Fates, you should have felt him," I said. "It was gross. I can't remember him, but I remember that power. That feeling."

"Oh, I felt him." Nix made a gagging noise.

"Same," Del said. "Won't forget that anytime soon."

"He was going to take me somewhere." The beer can crumpled in my hand.

"Back there?" Nix asked.

In a second, my mind was back in the cold dark of the cell from my nightmares. My breath caught, making it harder to suck in air.

Warmth settled over my shoulders. I shook my head and glanced down. Del's arm was wrapped around me, Nix's hand on my knee. I sighed and leaned into them.

"Maybe," I said, then shuddered. "Fates, he might have thrown Amara in there."

"There might be other girls in there." Nix's voice sounded lost.

"But why? What the hell does he want, besides the Heartstone and Amara?" Del asked.

I glanced down the hallway that led through my trove, straight back to the safe where I kept the scroll and the chalice.

"The names of more FireSouls from the Scroll of Truths," I said, thinking back to what Aaron had told me.

"And the Chalice of Youth," Nix said. "But that thing must do more than just make you look young, even though that's all the records say it does."

"I must have missed something in the research," Del said.

"We'll figure it out. But whatever his end game, it seems he's trying to collect strong magic," I said.

"He's succeeded in getting the Heartstone. If he finds a child with the gift to control it, then he can use it. The Alpha Council will protect Amara, but we can't let him get the scroll or the Chalice of Youth," Del said. "It's hidden in your trove, but the protections aren't great."

"We should probably spend some of that four mil on more protection spells for our troves and our shop," I said. Though it would be hard not to immediately spend it filling up my trove. My fingertips itched with the compulsion.

"Yeah. And maybe try to beef up the concealment charms that hide us. But in the meantime, you should give the scroll and chalice to Aidan," Nix said. "I had my doubts about him for a while, but he's *clearly* on our side. I trust him to know about us if he reads the scroll. And he's the best at protecting stuff, considering it's his freaking job."

I dropped my head back against the wall. Nix was right. Aidan would have to be pulling a really long, dangerous con on me if he was planning to betray me. My issues with him were more about my own fear than anything he'd done.

"Yeah, I'll give it to him," I said. "But that doesn't solve our problem. The Monster is hunting us. The concealment charms we bought five years ago will keep hiding us from an active search, but I don't trust that we won't run into him somehow."

"I'll try to figure out why I can turn into a phantom and if there's any way I can use it to help us," Del said. "Ever since I changed for the first time a week ago, I've just been adjusting to it. But I haven't tried to figure out why, besides chatting with those ghosts at the ruins."

"I think we gotta tell Connor and Claire what's up," Nix said. "If our concealment charms ever fail and the Monster does find us, they could be in the crossfire. They need to know what they're getting themselves into by being friends with us."

Guilt streaked through me and I winced. I didn't think they'd seen me take the Shifter's power at the ruins, but the memory of them fighting on our behalf raced through my mind. It should have been an easy battle, but it'd thrown them right into the path of the Monster.

"Agreed," I said. "They won't turn us in. We've been friends too long for that. We need to tell them we're going to keep our distance until this thing with the Monster blows over." *If it did.*

"They might quit being our friends anyway," Nix said.

"Which is fair," Del said. "We'd be asking them to risk a lot. Even if we get rid of the Monster, they'd be harboring known FireSouls. That's punishable by a stint in the Prison for Magical Miscreants."

An image of the shackled FireSoul being led down the hallway at the Alpha Council flashed in my mind.

"Yeah. We'll tell them tomorrow," I said. "Give them an out."

It had to be done, but I wasn't looking forward to it.

Early the next morning, I ambled down the street toward Potions & Pastilles. The sun was bright and cheerful, the birds chirping, and the morning looking like it'd turn into a beautiful Oregon summer day. The slight chill in the air would be banished by the sun and cats would laze on the grass.

And I would try not to lose my friends.

P & P was empty when I pushed open the door. Factory Row didn't get the kind of early-morning traffic that the business district got, so though Connor opened their doors at seven, customers didn't usually show until closer to eight.

Which was what I'd been counting on.

I turned on my newly acquired wolf Shifter senses when I walked in, just to try them out, and found that it was the easiest thing in the world. Just the matter of a thought. I hardly had to reach for my magic at all. Which was a good thing, since it meant I wouldn't give off much of a signature for a powerful supernatural to sense.

The smell of roasting coffee and baking cinnamon buns hit me about twenty times stronger than normal, thanks to my heightened senses. Nice. But I could also smell the trash and the bathroom, which wasn't so nice.

I turned off the senses as Connor looked up from behind the counter and grinned. His black band T-shirt was spotted with puffs of white flour.

"Hey! This is a bit early for you," he said.

"Yeah, guess it is." I eyed him loading the glass case with pastries. I could hear Claire in the kitchen, doing an early shift as I'd expected. "Whatcha got there?"

"Cinnamon buns." He pulled one out and showed me. The shiny white icing threatened to drip off the sides.

"Gimme." I made grabby hands as I approached and he handed it over. I didn't have to confess what I was until Nix and Del showed up, so I was going to take these last few minutes with my friend.

I bit into the cinnamon bun. Butter and sugar exploded over my taste buds.

"Amaything," I said, trying to keep my mouth closed as I chewed.

"My specialty. Want a latte?"

"Double boosted. I'm still dragging from these last few days." The boost was magic, but I didn't know what kind. Connor's specialty. He was as much a potion master as he was a Hearth Witch.

"So, you got plans this weekend?" I asked as he crafted my latte.

"Yeah, gonna check out the concert at the park. You want to come?"

"Might, yeah." Except I couldn't, because we wouldn't be friends then.

We spent the next ten minutes chatting about the live music that would be playing at the park. When the door behind me opened and Nix's and Del's voices drifted in, I stiffened. This was it.

"Hey, Connor, can you go get your sister?" I asked. Might as well pull this band aid off, especially since we couldn't do it if any other customers showed up.

"Uh, sure."

Nix and Del joined me at the barstools on either side, filling up the small counter.

"Now or never, eh?" Del said.

"Yeah." I gripped my mug.

Claire followed her brother out of the kitchen a moment later. She wore her leather fighting pants, but had pulled an apron over her black T-shirt. So she was pulling a double today—baker and mercenary.

She shoved her hair away from her face with her wrist. Her hands were still covered in flour. "Hey guys, what's up?"

Oh, not much. Just here to drop the bomb that obliterates our friendship.

"Uh, we had something we needed to tell you," I said instead.

"Yeah?" Connor asked.

"We're FireSouls," Del blurted out.

"But we're not evil," Nix added.

The air left the room. Any hope I'd had that they had already known and were cool with it, like Aidan had been, disappeared at the sight of their expressions.

They both looked like they'd been shot.

"FireSouls?" Claire whispered.

Connor shoved a hand through his messy hair. Then did it again. And again. "Shit."

Goosebumps crawled over my skin, nerves chasing nerves on top of nerves.

"Maybe you should tell us more," Claire said.

I sucked in a deep breath and started talking. The words fell off my tongue—our first memories as fifteen-year-olds, my nightmares, the Monster, his plans.

Their faces stayed the same throughout, as if they were trying to process and weren't thrilled with what they were hearing.

Who would be?

Hey, your closest friends are wanted by the law and hunted by a madman. Sign me up, said no one ever.

"So it would be dangerous for you if we keep being friends," Del said. "Which is why we can't be friends anymore, as I'm sure you can see."

Her voice sounded like shit. I felt like shit. Nix looked like shit, her jaw tense and her under-eyes baggy from exhaustion. We were the shit club.

Claire suddenly scowled. "Uh, actually I don't see that."

"It could just be temporary," I said, desperate to salvage anything I could.

"The hell it could," Connor said. "We're your friends. We've been friends for five years. My sister is a badass mercenary and I'm not exactly bad with a potion bomb myself. We're not going to just drop you when things get tough. What the hell kind of people do you think we are?"

I flinched. Connor sounded *mad*. But Connor didn't get mad. He was the chill one of the two.

"I'm sorry we didn't tell you sooner." I wanted to sink into the floor and live there.

"Yeah, me too," Claire said. "We could have had your back a lot sooner."

My gaze darted to hers.

"Don't look so freaking surprised." Claire scowled. "Like Connor said, what kind of friends do you think we are? You think we're going to drop you? Or that you can just waltz in here and say you're going to be all noble and shit and cut ties? Frankly, it's rude."

"Uh...."

"Well, we're not having it. You'd have our backs if stuff went to hell in our lives, so we've got your backs."

I glanced at Del and Nix. My shock was reflected in their gazes. Then I felt like shit for doubting my friends. For ever thinking they'd put up with this. I wouldn't ditch them, after all, so why would they ditch me?

"I'm sorry," I said, digging my fingers into the counter. "You're totally right. It was shitty of us to think you'd go for this. We were just trying to protect you, but I can see how insulting it was. To imply you would let us go it alone."

Connor slapped his palms on the counter. "Self-awareness for the win!" Then his expression softened. "Thanks for getting it. I appreciate the gesture. You guys were coming from a good place."

Claire gave us all a sharp look. "But don't think you can ever waltz in here again and break up with us. We're not having it. We're in this together, whatever it is."

My eyes prickled, then burned. I could feel my chin scrunching up as tears fell. I was one lucky freaking FireSoul.

CHAPTER FIFTEEN

"So, this is an interesting place to meet."

Aidan's deep voice sounded from behind me. I scrambled to my feet in the dark passageway and turned. He stood at the entrance to the tunnel that led into the Mayan pyramid, the bright sun shining at his back and sending all his features into shadow.

I dusted my hands off on my jeans and looked down at the floor, to where I'd just finished putting the broken stone back into place. It was the floor I'd blown apart with my lightning bolt when I'd been trying to keep the demon jaguars from eating us a week ago, before all this Amara stuff had happened.

"Yeah," I said. "I had to return the original diadem." Though I'd itched to put it in my trove. It would have look so good there. "And I wanted to fix this and figured you'd help me."

"So you sent me a message to meet you here?"

"I figured you'd come."

"You were right. But this was a long way to travel on public transport when you know I'd have taken you."

"Yeah, I needed some time to think." I could finally make out his features. He was more than just a pretty face to me now. He was the guy who'd had my back on more occasions than I could count, who'd healed me when I was sick. Who'd shared the darker parts of his past with me.

He was the guy who'd convinced me to open up to him, something I'd thought impossible.

"So, you still want that date?" I asked.

"Yeah." His voice was rougher than before.

I grinned. "Cool. If you'll let me borrow your Elemental Mage powers so I can meld this stone back together, you can pick the place."

"You know you can always mirror my powers. You don't need to ask."

"I know."

"Oh. *Oh.*" Understanding lit his voice. He spread his arms until they butted against the walls of the passage. "Have at it."

"Thanks." It was easier to reach for his magic now. Calling mine up from deep within came quicker, and finding his magical signature came easier as well. I felt the grit of stone beneath my fingertips as I let the power flow from me to the stone floor.

A golden light glowed, highlighting the cracks in the rock as I forced magic into it. The fissures gradually faded until the stone was solid once more. Original.

I smiled and stepped back. "There. All better."

"Why do you care so much?"

I turned to face him. "These ancient sites are one of a kind. They're pieces of the past that tell stories about people who are no longer here. About living peoples' ancestors. It's important to preserve them."

"Of course. But it seems personal to you. Less than two days ago, you were in the biggest battle of your life. And the first thing you do is come down here and fix this damage?"

I shrugged. "I guess that since I can't remember my past, history has taken on a greater significance for me. I don't know. I don't want to analyze it. It's just important to me."

"Your past." His tone was gentle but prodding, and I supposed it was time I let him in on some of it. What little I knew.

"Come on. Let's go outside," I said.

He squinted at me, then turned and walked out into the bright sun. The heat hit me immediately, but it was nice. I turned left, toward the long line of steps climbing to the top of the pyramid, and began to ascend. About fifteen feet up, I turned and sat, facing the jungle. Brilliant green foliage rustled in the light breeze.

Aidan climbed to join me, his dark gray shirt stark against the riot of green behind him. I could make out the strap of a small dark bag slung across his back. Like a manly, cross-body backpack.

He settled down next to me.

"So, the Monster that hunts us," I said. "I've never told you about my past with him. What little I remember of it."

"You haven't trusted me yet."

"I guess not. Not trusting has been the most effective tool in my arsenal."

"Fair enough. But you trust me now?"

His past deeds flashed before my eyes, one after the other like those stereograph toys that kids used to play with in the old days. "You've kind of given me no choice by being so honorable and helpful and all that."

He grinned, his white teeth flashing. "Sorry about that."

I punched him lightly on the arm. "You should be. I had my plan all worked out. Keep the truth limited to my *deirfiúr*. Two friends, max."

"Connor and Claire."

"Yeah." Just hearing their names made me grin. "It was working out great. Then you showed up."

"Along with trouble."

"Trouble, like the Monster, trouble?"

He nodded.

"I guess you're right. You and he showed up in my life at the same time. That might have been one reason I subconsciously didn't trust you. But I think it was mostly a lifetime of thinking everyone was out to get me." I laughed, not entirely joyfully. "What can I say? Victim complex!"

"Hardly."

I reached over and grabbed his hand, wowed anew by how big he was. I glanced down at our joined palms. His was so broad and strong-looking. But physical strength wasn't everything.

As he'd proven by helping me find my own power. True, he'd had to blackmail me into practicing by threatening to tell the Order of the Magica about me, but he'd done it because he cared about me. Because he wanted me to be safe.

"You've done really well with your magic this last week," he said.

"Thanks. But I need a lot more work. Both controlling my magic and my signature."

"At least you're now committed to trying."

"I am. But sorry I was so damned stubborn about it at first."

"No surprise you were. But you were right to be afraid. Most supernaturals would turn you over in a heartbeat, like Mathias almost did."

I thought of Claire and Connor, who hadn't ditched us.

"And you need to keep being careful," Aidan said. "Stick to using your magic in abandoned tombs and practice so you can suppress your signature. When Angus said your magic smelled strange, I almost had a damned heart attack."

"Yeah. The Shifters having just caught a FireSoul didn't help. Thank fates they didn't connect us." Besides Mathias. "And you're right, I'll keep practicing. I need to be able to pass off my new FireSoul powers as borrowed Mirror Mage abilities."

He squeezed my hand. "I'll help you."

"Thanks." I sucked in a deep breath. "I suppose in return I should tell you about my past. What little I know."

"I wouldn't turn that down."

I nodded, then started with my first memories—the ones from the nightmares. Aidan's hand tightened on mine at times, particularly those when I'd been in danger. He really didn't like the story about me attacking the guard, but his grip had loosened when the guard finally lay dead.

"Do you know what happened after that?" he asked.

"No. Nightmare stopped. Next thing I remember is waking up in the field with Nix and Del when we were fifteen." I told him all about that, and the next ten years, half of which had been spent running and hiding, the next half spent just plain hiding, thanks to our concealment charms.

"You're one tough Magica," Aidan said when I finally trailed off.

"Haven't had much choice." But I was secretly pleased by my capability. And his praise.

"That's what makes you tough. You could have curled up and died. Or hid out in a mountain like a hermit."

"I'm a beach girl."

He grinned, then dragged his bag off his back and unzipped it. He pulled out a slim box and handed it to me. "For you."

My gaze darted between the box and his eyes. "Yeah?"

"Yeah."

I opened the box. Two obsidian daggers lay inside. Replacements for Lefty and Righty, who I'd incinerated in my magic when I'd shifted. I'd bet they were enchanted to return to me when I called, just like the last pair.

My heart warmed. "Thanks. These are rare."

"Yeah. I'm going to have to start looking farther afield when you lose this pair."

"I didn't lose the first pair. I sacrificed a dagger to help find the Scroll of Truths, if you'll recall." Which reminded me. "By the way, the scroll wasn't lost in the lightning on the island. I've got it."

"Can't say I'm surprised."

"I want to give it to you for safe keeping. That, and the Chalice of Youth. I think the Monster wants them for something. We can't let him have them. Whatever your best security is, these objects need it."

"I'll protect them." His gaze met mine, serious and determined. "Just like I'll protect you."

"Thank you." I leaned in to kiss him.

I appreciated that he would try. But I had a feeling that protecting myself was a job only I could do. And I was determined to do it.

THANK YOU FOR READING!

I hoped you liked *Mirror Mage*. Reviews are *so* helpful to authors. I really appreciate all reviews, both positive and negative.

The sequel to *Mirror Mage* will be available in June. Join my newsletter to find out more. I love hearing from readers. You can contact me at Linsey@LinseyHall.com.

If you'd like to know more about the inspiration for the Dragon's Gift series, please read on for the Author's Note.

AUTHOR'S NOTE

Hey, there! I hope you enjoyed reading *Mirror Mage* as much as I enjoyed writing it. The Dragon's Gift series has really become a labor of love for me because I am also an archaeologist. This series allows me to combine my two loves—writing and history—which has been massively fun.

As with my other books, I included historical sites in *Mirror Mage*. The most important historical site in *Mirror Mage* is the ruined city that is the setting for the final battle. This took place at the ruins of Ephesus, the ancient Greek and Roman city in Turkey. The statue of Hercules, the ampitheatre, the library, the brothel, and even the sign pointing to the brothel are all real. You can even visit! I haven't had the pleasure myself, but a colleague of mine, Dr. Ayse Devrim Atauz, helped me understand the layout and feel of the city. Any errors are my own (or were made to improve the story, like moving the amphitheater slightly).

But one of the most important things about the Dragon's Gift series is Cass's relationship with the artifacts and the sense of responsibility she feels to protect them. I spoke about this in the Author's Note for *Ancient Magic*, so this might be repetitive for some folks (feel free to quit now if so), but I want to include it in each of my Author's Notes because it's so important to me.

I knew I had a careful line to tread when writing these books—combining the ethics of archaeology with the fantasy aspect of treasure hunting isn't always easy.

There is a big difference between these two activities. As much as I value artifacts, they are not treasure. Not even the gold artifacts. They are pieces of our history that contain valuable information, and as such, they belong to all of us. Every artifact that is excavated should be properly conserved and stored in a museum so that everyone can have access to our history. No one single person can own history, and I believe very strongly that individuals should not own artifacts. Treasure hunting is the pursuit of artifacts for personal gain.

So why did I make Cass Cleraux a treasure hunter? I'd have loved to call her an archaeologist, but nothing about Cass's work is like archaeology. Archaeology is a very laborious, painstaking process—and it certainly doesn't involve selling artifacts. That wouldn't work for the fast paced, adventurous series that I had planned for Dragon's Gift. Not to mention the fact that dragons are famous for coveting treasure. Considering where Cass got her skills from, it just made sense to call her a treasure hunter (though I really like to think of her as a magic hunter). Even though I write urban fantasy, I strive for accuracy. Cass doesn't engage in archaeological practices—therefore, I cannot call her an archaeologist. I also have a duty as an archaeologist to properly represent my field and our goals—namely, to protect and share history. Treasure hunting doesn't do this. One of the biggest battles that archaeology faces today is protecting cultural heritage from thieves.

I debated long and hard about not only what to call Cass, but also about how she would do her job. I wanted it to involve all the cool things we think about when we think about archaeology—namely, the Indiana Jones stuff, whether it's real or not. Because that stuff is fun, and my main goal is to write a fun book. But I didn't know quite how to do that while still staying within the bounds of my own ethics. I can cut myself and other writers some slack because this is fiction, but I couldn't go too far into smash and grab treasure hunting.

I consulted some of my archaeology colleagues to get their take, which was immensely helpful. Wayne Lusardi, the State Maritime Archaeologist for Michigan, and Douglas Inglis and Veronica Morris, both archaeologists for Interactive Heritage, were immensely helpful with ideas. My biggest problem was figuring out how to have Cass steal artifacts from tombs and then sell them and still sleep at night. Everything I've just said is pretty counter to this, right?

That's where the magic comes in. Cass isn't after the artifacts themselves (she puts them back where she found them, if you recall)—she's after the magic that the artifacts contain. She's more of a magic hunter than a treasure hunter. That solved a big part of my problem. At least she was putting the artifacts back. Though that's not proper archaeology (especially the damage she sometimes causes, which she always goes back to fix), I could let it pass. At least it's clear that she believes she shouldn't keep the artifact or harm the site. But the SuperNerd in me said, "Well, that magic is part of the artifact's context. It's important to the artifact and shouldn't be removed and sold."

Now *that* was a problem. I couldn't escape my SuperNerd self, so I was in a real conundrum. Fortunately, that's where the immensely intelligent Wayne Lusardi came in. He suggested that the magic could have an expiration date. If the magic wasn't used before it decayed, it could cause huge problems. Think explosions and tornado spells run amok. It could ruin the entire site, not to mention possibly cause injury and death. That would be very bad.

So now you see why Cass Clereaux didn't just steal artifacts to sell them. Not only is selling the magic cooler, it's also better from an ethical standpoint, especially if the magic was going to cause problems in the long run. These aren't perfect solutions—the perfect solution would be sending in a team of archaeologists to carefully record the site and remove the dangerous magic—but that wouldn't be a very fun book. Hopefully this was a good compromise that you enjoyed (and that my old professors don't hang their heads over).

ABOUT LINSEY

Before becoming a writer, Linsey was an archaeologist who studied shipwrecks in all kinds of water, from the tropics to muddy rivers (and she has a distinct preference for one over the other). After a decade of tromping around in search of old bits of stuff, she settled down to started penning her own adventure novels and is freaking delighted that people seem to like them. Since life is better with a little (or a lot of) magic, she writes urban fantasy and paranormal romance.

This is a work of fiction. All reference to events, persons, and locale are used fictitiously, except where documented in historical record. Names, characters, and places are products of the author's imagination, and any resemblance to actual events, locales, or persons, living or dead, is coincidental.

Copyright 2016 by Linsey Hall
Published by Bonnie Doon Press LLC

All rights reserved, including the right of reproduction in whole or in part in any form, except in instances of quotation used in critical articles or book review. Where such permission is sufficient, the author grants the right to strip any DRM which may be applied to this work.

Linsey@LinseyHall.com
www.LinseyHall.com
https://twitter.com/HiLinseyHall
https://www.facebook.com/LinseyHallAuthor

BONNIE
DOON
PRESS

ISBN 978-1-942085-16-4

CPSIA information can be obtained
at www.ICGtesting.com
Printed in the USA
LVOW12s1507140716
496335LV00001B/98/P